Dirty Sexy Cuffed

NEW YORK TIMES BESTSELLING AUTHORS

Carly Phillips

Erika Wilde

CARLYPHILLIPS.COM
ERIKAWILDE.COM

**"The love story Phillips and Wilde crafted was rare, dipped in a reality so natural and organic it held my heart from the very first page."
~ Audrey Carlan, #1 New York Times Bestselling Author**

New York Times bestselling authors Carly Phillips and Erika Wilde bring you a dirty, sexy, smoking hot series featuring three bad boy brothers bonded by shocking secrets and their damaged past. Sinful, addicting, and unapologetically alpha, these men are every woman's erotic daydream . . . And your ultimate dirty fantasy.

Are you ready to get Cuffed?

As a cop, Levi Kincaid is all about discipline and control . . .in the bedroom, and out of it, and he's always been very careful about choosing women who abide by his rules. Hot sex and intense pleasure? No problem. Emotional commitment and forever promises? No way. But he never anticipates falling for a blue eyed angel who makes him want to cuff her to his bed and do dirty, sexy things to her. And that control of his? It doesn't stand a chance against Sarah Robins, the one woman he can't resist . . .

* * *

Chapter One

"**S**O, WHAT'LL IT be for dinner? Chicken or beef ramen?" Sarah Robins considered both of the Styrofoam cups of noodles she held in her hands—her last two choices for a decent meal before she headed out to work for the night.

Thank God tomorrow was payday so she could make a trip to Walmart and stock up on her staples— ramen, oatmeal, bread, peanut butter and jelly, fruit, and bottled water. Those were the basics she lived on. After she paid her by-the-week motel bill, she was left with around fifty dollars for all her other expenses, including groceries and toiletries.

She'd spent the past five weeks budgeting her money very carefully while also trying to save whatever was left after purchasing only the necessities she needed to get by on. Working twenty-five hours a week for minimum wage at a convenience store and gas station wasn't ideal. Neither were her swing shift hours that meant she didn't get off until midnight. But for now, it was a desperately needed job, and she'd do whatever it took to get back on her feet so she could finally leave the city that had brought her nothing but heartache.

Exhaling a deep breath and refusing to dwell on the painful memories of the past, Sarah decided on the chicken ramen. After opening a bottle of water, she filled a ceramic mug and put it into the small, compact microwave she'd bought at a second-hand store. A minute and a half later, she poured the boiling-hot water into the ramen and closed the lid to let it steam while she finished getting ready for work. She pulled on a pair of well worn jeans, a plain T-shirt, and sneakers. Makeup was a luxury she couldn't afford, so she washed and moisturized her face, then put her hair into a ponytail.

Her stomach growled hungrily, and she picked up her soup and sat down on the bed to eat. Her motel room was small, with just a queen-sized bed, dresser, closet, and bathroom, but it was all she needed for now. And even if the Sleepy Time Motel catered to a less-than-savory clientele who tended to pay for a room by the hour, it was better than the nights she'd spent at the homeless shelter or on the streets. She was grateful she had a place to lay her head every night, with a door that securely locked and bolted, until she was ready to move on.

Her end goal was to make a new life for herself anyplace other than Chicago. She needed to leave here, and soon, because it was just a matter of time before her possessive ex-boyfriend, Dylan, found her. And there was no doubt in Sarah's mind that he *was* looking for her. It was hard to forget how he'd threatened to come after her if she ever left him or if she escaped the cult-like compound where they'd lived for nearly three weeks.

A shiver stole through her when she thought about where, exactly, her life had been headed and what she'd been expected to do while living in the gated community. She considered herself lucky she'd managed to get out with just the clothes on her back and a little over fifty dollars in her pocket. But she was now considered a deserter—a punishable offense according to the rules of the Sacrosanct community—which was why she was keeping a low profile and saving everything she could to start over somewhere far away.

This time, she was determined to get it right. To be strong and independent, without relying on a man for anything. She was finished letting her insecurities rule her emotions, and she was done getting involved with the kind of guys who were only out for themselves and ended up using her for their own purposes, like the situation with Dylan that she'd narrowly escaped. The future was all about finally putting the past, and her bad choices, behind her, and she was looking forward to a clean slate.

Finished with her meal, Sarah glanced at the clock on the dresser. The bus would be at her stop in twenty minutes, so she headed out the door and into the early evening dusk. The motel's parking lot was already alive with activity for a Tuesday night, and Sarah did her best to hold her head up high without making any eye contact with the sleazy men who were there to either score drugs or a prostitute. She was thankful the bus stop was less than a block down the road, but that didn't stop her from clutching her compact-size mace in her hand.

Once she was settled on the bus, she relaxed for a bit, though she was always keenly aware of her surroundings, especially in this area. She honestly couldn't wait until she could leave this town and her job at Circle K, and she reminded herself that every day at work brought her that much closer to leaving it all behind.

There was one thing she'd miss once she moved on, though—or rather, one particular person, she thought with a private smile—and that was Levi Kincaid. The gorgeous, hot cop with light green eyes that made her think of the sea glass she'd used to find at the beach when she was a young girl, before she'd lost her entire family to a house fire. Another painful part of her past she didn't like to dwell on. She much preferred thinking about Levi.

Over the past five weeks, he'd made a habit of stopping at the convenience store around eleven thirty at night with his partner, right before his shift ended—to get a drink and late-night snack for the ride back to the station, or so he claimed. But considering his flirty comments and his blatant interest, she suspected it was all an excuse to see her. He'd even asked her out a few times, but as attracted as she was, and as tempted as he made her *feel*, she knew the timing was all wrong, and she'd turned him down every single time.

His attention was flattering, especially since she wasn't one of those beautiful, confident girls who typically turned a man's head. At least, not a man as devastatingly sexy as Levi. She was plain and ordinary and certainly nothing special. But for the handful of minutes that Levi spent in the store, charming her with his smile and words, she imagined that she *was* someone special.

Levi Kincaid was the best part of her night, the one exciting thing she had to look forward to. And she was going to miss him when she was gone.

"WHEN ARE YOU going to face the fact that this chick just isn't into you?"

Levi Kincaid glanced across the dark interior of the unmarked SUV to his partner, Nick Catalano, who was alternating his attention between navigating the road and making sure Levi saw his smartass smirk. It wasn't the first time his friend had given Levi shit about his request to stop by Circle K on their way back to the station after their shift ended.

For the past two months, they'd been assigned to the DUI Strike Force in the area, which made stopping by the mart convenient. Seeing and flirting with Sarah Robins was just a bonus.

"She's totally into me, so that's not the issue," Levi refuted confidently, not at all bothered by Nick's ribbing. There were many times he'd caught the tempting way Sarah looked at him when she didn't think he was aware of her. And there was no mistaking the attraction between them she was so determined to fight. He just hadn't figured out *why* yet. But he would.

"Then what's the problem?" Nick persisted—this from a man who was all about instant gratification when it came to women, while Levi was more . . . selective.

"I'm not sure yet," he replied honestly.

Truthfully, he was having a hell of a time getting past that wariness of hers, which only made him more curious about who Sarah Robins was—and where she'd come from. Admittedly, his interest in her had nothing to do with him being an inquisitive cop and everything to do with him wanting her, in a deeper way than any female had gotten to him before. He just had to get *her* on the same page as him.

Levi wasn't normally the type of guy who'd continue to pursue a woman who'd already turned him down half a dozen times. A smart man would have cut his losses after the first rejection, but from the moment he'd looked into Sarah's sweet, soulful blue eyes, he'd felt a connection that only seemed to grow stronger every time he saw her.

And he certainly didn't miss the irony of that realization, when he was a man adept at maintaining strict control of his emotions—in all aspects of his life.

"This is a shit part of town," Nick said, stating the obvious, which brought Levi's thoughts back to the present. "As soon as we're off this DUI task force, I don't want to drive through this part of Englewood unless it's for a call, so close the deal with Sarah already."

"Winning a woman over takes time, Catalano," Levi said easily—especially one as wary as Sarah. "Though that's something I wouldn't expect you to understand."

"Hell no," he agreed with a quick player's grin. "That's too much fucking work when there are plenty of women who take one look at this uniform and are instantly willing and eager to bend over and drop their panties. Trust me, getting laid, and regularly, is not an issue for me."

Levi had plenty of offers; he was just more particular about his bed partners. He didn't do one-night stands, but he didn't do long-term committed, either. The few women he'd dated and allowed into his private life were looking for the same thing he was—a mutually satisfying physical relationship without any emotional involvement. More importantly, they were willing to let him be in control during all aspects of sex.

And Sarah, from everything he'd learned so far, didn't strike him as the type looking for long term, either. Which made his pursuit easier for him to justify . . . and live with.

Arriving at the Circle K, Nick turned the SUV into

the deserted lot. He drove past the gas station area and stopped in front of the convenience store instead of parking the vehicle.

"I noticed the back tire was low at the DUI check point," Nick said, explaining why he hadn't pulled into one of the many empty spaces in front of the mart like he normally did. "While you run inside and do your thing, I'm going to drive around back and fill the tire up with air. I'll meet you out front when you're done."

"Sounds good." Levi released his seat belt and opened the door. "You want anything?"

Nick grinned. "Yeah, I'll take a root beer and a Snickers bar."

"You got it." Levi hopped out of the truck, and while his partner drove off and disappeared behind the building, he headed toward the store.

Out of years of habit, he glanced around the area, looking for anything, or anyone, who might be out of place. Especially in this part of town. But it was a quiet evening, and there weren't any other cars or people around, which wasn't unusual for a late Tuesday night. He walked into the store, and to his immediate left was the main counter and two registers. Sarah was sitting on a stool reading a magazine, and as soon as she heard someone enter, she looked up.

Her bored expression immediately transformed to one of pleasure as a genuine, happy-to-see-him smile curved her soft, lush mouth, which never failed to make him think about slowly licking his tongue across that full lower lip before kissing her, or how that mouth would feel sliding down the length of his cock as she looked up at him from a kneeling position on the floor at his feet.

Heat and desire mingled in his belly and lower as he strolled toward the counter. Yeah, he'd stored up five long weeks' worth of the hottest, most sinful fantasies of Sarah, in some of the most erotic scenarios he could imagine. Those dirty thoughts had come in handy when he'd lain in bed, hard and aching and needing relief. With his hand wrapped tight around his dick, those decadent visions playing through his mind never failed to alleviate his lust.

But the relief was always temporary. He wanted the real thing. He wanted Sarah, her body soft and warm beneath his, and her willing to give herself over to him in all the ways he desired. And that kind of trust took time. And patience. Both of which he had in abundance.

Setting the magazine aside, she moved off her chair and stood on the opposite side of the counter from him. She was wearing a plain T-shirt and worn jeans, and it wasn't the first time that he had the thought that her body was almost too slender for her frame. Which made him want to cook her a carb-loaded meal, just to watch her eat and put on a few extra pounds to fill out her curves.

With her light brown hair pulled into a ponytail—he'd never seen it any other way—her delicate features were more prominent, her eyes bigger and bluer. She wasn't one of those gorgeous, made-up women, but that was more Nick's type than his. Rather, she was pretty in a way that was all natural, her complexion soft and smooth with a hint of pink from the light blush sweeping across her cheeks.

She absently ran her tongue along her bottom lip, her clear, sky-blue eyes taking in his appearance just as openly. "Good evening, Officer Kincaid."

Officer Kincaid. He liked the way that sounded in her soft, husky tone. His dick liked it, too, and he suddenly wanted to hear that breathless voice in a much more intimate setting. Like his bedroom. Preferably with her naked, restrained, and begging him for what she wanted and needed.

Another surge of awareness hummed through his body, and he wiped those sexy thoughts from his mind before they got him in trouble. "Hi, Sarah," he said, smiling at her. "How are things tonight?"

"Quiet and slow," she replied with a small shrug. "You're the first customer I've had in the past hour."

"Where's Robby?" he asked as he casually glanced around the front end of the store for the guy who usually worked the night shift with her. Knowing that she wasn't completely alone and vulnerable to any asshole who might come into the store had always made Levi feel marginally better.

She shifted on her feet. "He went home about a half hour ago. He wasn't feeling well and said he felt like he was coming down with the flu. The last thing I need is to catch whatever he's got, so I told him to leave."

The crime rate in this lower-income part of the city was significant, with late-night marts being a prime source of robberies. He frowned at her, his protective instincts automatically rising, though they felt a helluva lot stronger when it came to *her* safety than just a cop's concern. "So you're here all by yourself?"

"Yes," she said with an amused laugh.

When he crossed his arms over his chest and didn't crack a smile, she realized how serious he was about the situation.

"It's really not a big deal, Levi," she rushed to assure him. "There's only twenty minutes left until graveyard shift comes in and relieves me and I can go home. I'm not going to be here by myself for much longer. And it's not like we have a mad rush of customers tonight."

That wasn't the point, but Levi let the issue go, considering her co-workers would be there soon enough. Instead, he leaned a hip against the counter and moved on to a different and more personal topic. The one that usually ended with a rejection. It was a good thing he didn't have a fragile ego.

"So, any plans for the coming weekend?" he asked as he casually hooked his thumbs into the utility belt around his waist. "Saturday, specifically?"

The corner of her mouth quirked slightly at his indirect way of asking her out. "Just working."

He tipped his head curiously. "No days off?"

She hesitated for a moment before responding. "I do have Sunday off, but that's my day to do stuff."

Stuff. Which sounded like an excuse to him.

"What about fun?" he countered easily. "Ever take time for that?"

"It's been awhile," she admitted softly.

He didn't miss the quick flicker of sadness in her gaze that made him want to reach out and touch her, to use his thumb to smooth away the crease that had formed between her brows. Resisting the urge took more effort than he'd expected. "Then how about you say yes to a date with me, and I'll remedy that for you. I'm all about having a good time with a pretty girl," he added with a wink.

She opened her mouth to speak, and certain a denial was about to spill out, he quickly held up a hand to stop her. "Wait. Don't say anything." She pressed her lips back together, and even though her gaze was wary, he continued on while he still had a bit of leverage. "I want you to *really* think about your answer this time, instead of automatically turning me down, because one more rejection might just crush me."

Light laughter escaped her. "I truly doubt that."

He leaned across the counter so he was a bit closer. "But do you *really* want to take that chance?" he teased.

He'd meant to make her laugh again, so that she'd lower her guard a little more. But instead, her doubtful gaze searched his expression, looking for answers he didn't know the questions to until she finally asked.

"Why me?"

The uncertainty in her voice caught him by surprise, but his response was immediate and sincere. "Why *not* you?"

"Because girls like me . . ." She shook her head and glanced away, but not before he saw the pained look in her eyes. "Never mind."

He wasn't going to let her off so easy. Not with a statement like that. "Girls like you . . . what?" he persisted.

She released an exasperated sigh and met his gaze again. "I just think you and I come from different worlds, or opposite sides of the city, as the case may be."

He arched a brow. "And you're basing that assumption on what, exactly? Me being a cop?"

"Yes," she replied with a nod.

Little did she know, the respectable image he presented to the public as a police officer hid a wealth of deep, dark secrets—along with a past that was grim and twisted and would undoubtedly horrify her if she knew the truth. It was those memories that reminded him much too often which side of the city he'd grown up in—the shitty, hellish side where he and his brothers had struggled every single day to survive.

But he didn't tell her any of that because it didn't matter in the scheme of wanting a date with her. Instead, he flashed her a persuasive smile. "Sweetheart, there's a whole lot more to me than just this uniform and my good looks," he teased. "But the only way you're going to find out who I am *out* of this uniform is to say yes." And yeah, he'd deliberately given that comment a double meaning she clearly didn't miss. "So, just think about that for a few minutes, and when I come back, hopefully you'll give me a different answer."

He pushed away from the counter and walked down one of the snack aisles. But instead of getting Nick's Snickers bar and their drinks from the cooler, Levi headed toward the back of the store to use the men's restroom first. He took care of business, washed his hands, and just as he was drying them with a paper towel, he heard a loud male voice yelling from somewhere in the store.

Immediately concerned, he slipped from the restroom and moved silently down the hallway to assess the situation. He glanced around the corner and felt his stomach lurch when he saw a tall, lanky man in his mid-twenties up by the front counter, with a gun pointed directly at Sarah as she opened the cash register, the terror on her face nearly gutting Levi.

Jesus fucking Christ. With only seconds to make a decision, he moved back into the hallway and used his shoulder mic to report a 10-31, robbery in progress, to Nick and dispatch, then turned off the radio so the suspect wouldn't hear any response. Retrieving his gun from his holster, he ducked below the shelving to keep his presence concealed. Then, slowly, he moved toward the front of the store so he had a better vantage point before confronting the man. His heart pumped hard and fast in his chest, along with a rush of adrenaline, and all he could think about was Sarah and making sure she got out of this situation safely.

"All the money, *now*, bitch," the guy screamed like a crazed person hopped up on drugs. "You're going way too fucking slow, and if you don't hurry up I'm going to blow your fucking head off!"

He heard Sarah make a soft sound of distress, and knowing he at least had the element of surprise on his side, Levi stepped out into the open, gun raised, and pointed it at the man's chest. "Police, drop your gun!"

The suspect immediately turned at the sound of his voice, the weapon he was holding now aiming straight at Levi. The man's hand moved slightly, and without hesitating, Levi pulled his trigger just as the perp opened fire and two individual shots rang out.

The impact of the bullet striking Levi's body armor hurt like a motherfucker and forced him back a step. Somehow he managed to catch himself before he fell on his ass. The other man wasn't as fortunate. Levi's shot nailed the guy in his right shoulder, causing him to drop his gun as he screamed in pain.

Still reeling from the hit, Levi nevertheless moved to take the robber down, but Nick came barreling through the doors and beat him to it. Within seconds, his partner had the suspect face down on the ground and was securing him in cuffs, which gave Levi a moment to catch his breath, considering he felt as though he'd been hit in the rib cage by a baseball bat.

"Oh, my God, Levi!" Sarah rushed around the front counter, her face pale and her eyes wide with fear as she reached him. "He *shot* you. Are you okay?"

He secured his weapon in his holster and glanced down at the gaping hole in his ballistic vest and the slug buried in the Kevlar fibers. "Jesus," he muttered, shocked by the realization that yeah, *he'd been shot.* Which was quickly followed by gratitude for the armor that had most likely saved his life.

"I'll be okay," he said as he looked Sarah over thoroughly to make sure she wasn't injured in any way. "Did he hurt you at all?"

"No, I'm fine," she assured him, her quivering voice not as confident as her words. "Just shaken up."

His first instinct was to take care of Sarah, to get her out of this fucking convenience store that she shouldn't be working at in the first place, but he didn't have that luxury. He now had a crime scene to process, and knowing that Sarah was okay, his job was a priority.

"I know that was scary as hell, but I need you to stay behind the counter while we arrest the suspect and collect evidence," he told her as he heard Nick calling for EMT assistance on his shoulder mic. "And don't touch anything, okay?"

She nodded in understanding and did as Levi asked, giving him the ability to focus on the situation at hand. Within minutes, backup arrived, and the store was filled with police activity. The suspect was read his rights and taken out to one of the ambulances that had arrived to transport him to the hospital for treatment. Afterwards, he'd be taken to jail.

Levi started the paperwork part of the investigation.

"Hey, Ironman. In case it escaped your notice, you were shot," his partner said gruffly. "Despite the vest, you need to have the paramedics take a look and make sure you're okay."

"I'm good," he lied, deliberately ignoring the throbbing pain in his left side whenever he inhaled a deep breath. "I can still see the back end of the bullet, so I'm not dealing with an open wound." Besides, the sooner they wrapped up the crime scene and investigation, the sooner he could get Sarah out of here, since the two employees who worked the graveyard shift at the convenience mart had arrived. "Let's get this done and then I'll have the EMT check it out."

While Levi handled the crime scene and log, collected and recorded evidence, and had one of the other employees give him a copy of the surveillance video, Nick interviewed Sarah and wrote down her statement. An hour later, all the paperwork was complete, the area cleaned up, and Sarah was still exactly where Levi had told her to stay—sitting on the stool behind the front counter.

Levi walked around the counter. As he approached, he realized how exhausted she looked—and again, he experienced that inexplicable urge to take care of her—because she just looked so damn vulnerable after being held up at gunpoint.

All his life, he'd been surrounded by some form of violence—from childhood to the military to being in law enforcement—and a part of him was immune to most of the brutality in the world around him. But he was pretty damn sure that Sarah wasn't used to having her life threatened with a gun pointed at her head, and he hated that some doped-up asshole had changed all that for her.

He stopped right in front of the knees she'd pressed so primly together, and it was harder than hell not to push them apart so he could step even closer. "You ready to get out of here?" he asked.

She nodded eagerly, her expression grateful that she was finally being released. "Yes. Are you done with me?"

He allowed a sexy smile to curve his lips. Touching his fingers under her chin, he tipped her face up so he was looking directly into her wide eyes.

"Sweet, sweet Sarah. What a silly question," he chastised in a soft murmur so only she could hear. "You should know by now that I'm not even *close* to being done with you."

Chapter Two

SARAH STARED INTO Levi's light green eyes, mesmerized by the way they gradually darkened with desire. With nothing more than his gentle touch, he'd managed to diffuse her anxiety, but his softly spoken words—*I'm not even close to being done with you*—made her all too aware of him as a man. A sexy, gorgeous man who'd literally saved her life.

"Thank you," she whispered, knowing things could have ended very differently tonight if he hadn't stopped by the store.

"For?" he asked as he let his hand fall away.

"Protecting me." The only man who'd ever made her feel safe had been her father, and as a child, she'd been devastated when he'd died. The foster homes she'd lived in had taught her that the only person she could trust and rely on was herself. And the men she'd allowed into her life over the years since had only reinforced that realization.

"I'm just glad that I was here when it all went down," he said in a low, gruff voice.

"Me, too," she admitted. She shuddered to think what might have happened if she'd been alone.

"Kincaid!" Nick called out impatiently, causing Levi to look over his shoulder at his partner, who was standing just inside the store's double doors. "Get your ass out here. The EMT can't leave or sign off on your release until they examine you."

"Be right there." Levi glanced back at Sarah and rolled his eyes, his gaze filled with annoyance. "He's such a pain in the ass."

She laughed, then grew more serious. "I'm going to have to agree with him. You really need to make sure that you're okay."

"The shot probably caused nothing more than a bruise," he grumbled like a typical man, even as he gingerly touched the area where the bullet was still lodged in his vest.

"Then it shouldn't be an issue for you to let a paramedic look you over," she insisted. "And it would make me feel better, too."

He tipped his head to the side, looking adorably boyish instead of like the badass cop he'd just been. "Since you're now off the clock, care to accompany me out to the ambulance?"

"Sure." It was the least she could do for him, but before she could slide off the stool, he moved closer, keeping her in place.

"Don't think you're off the hook," he said, his

voice low and husky as he slowly dragged his heated gaze from her mouth back up to her eyes. "I haven't forgotten that you still owe me an answer."

She'd only known Levi for a few weeks, but it was enough time to realize that he wasn't a man who missed much or let things go easily, so it didn't surprise Sarah that he'd given her a little reminder of the date he'd asked her out on. He'd certainly given her a persuasive argument when she'd questioned his interest in her, but did she really want to get involved with Levi, in any way, when she was going to leave Chicago in a few weeks?

The woman who was insanely attracted to him was jumping up and down and yelling, *yes*! while the more practical, cautious side was quick to remind her that she didn't need the complication of having *any* man in her life right now. Her ex, Dylan, was complication enough.

After letting the graveyard shift know that she was leaving, she grabbed her purse and followed Levi outside to the ambulance, where an EMT was waiting for him. Not wanting to get in the way, Sarah stood off to the side while the paramedic asked him to remove his vest and shirt so he could get a better look at the bullet's point of impact.

Levi took off the utility belt around his waist that held his handcuffs, baton, and other equipment, then removed the heavy outer armor that had protected him from the suspect's bullet. He unbuttoned his uniform shirt and shrugged it off. Underneath, he wore a navy blue T-shirt, and when he stripped it over his head, Sarah found herself way too captivated with how freaking hot he looked half-naked. He was solidly built with broad shoulders and muscled arms, and his tight, defined abs were testament to regular workouts.

Holy smokes. If she thought he looked sexy and attractive in his uniform, he was devastatingly, breathtakingly gorgeous *out* of only half of it.

She was in complete and utter awe . . . until her gaze skimmed over the large bruise already forming on his rib cage. The area was swollen and discolored in a combination of red, blue, and purple hues, and when the technician gently touched the contusion, Levi winced and swore low and harsh.

The guy tending to him glanced up at Levi. "I need you to try and take a deep breath."

Levi attempted to fill his lungs with air but instead expelled an agonizing groan. "Shit, that fucking hurts."

He grimaced and clenched his jaw, and Sarah felt his pain, along with a jolt of guilt. It was difficult *not* to feel distressed, since Levi had been shot because he'd stopped by the store to visit *her*.

"I thought taking off the vest would relieve some of the pressure," he grumbled, his brows furrowing into a deeper line. "But now it feels worse, and especially when I inhale."

The EMT frowned. "Yeah, I'm pretty sure you've got a cracked or fractured rib," he said as he wrapped a blood-pressure cuff around Levi's upper arm to get his vitals. "But hey, on a positive note, you're still alive."

Levi chuckled, but Sarah didn't find the joke the least bit funny. Especially when he moaned again as he pressed a hand to his side, his features etched in unmistakable pain. She shifted anxiously on her feet, feeling helpless because there was nothing she could do while he was in such obvious misery.

Nick strolled up to the group. "So, is Ironman going to survive?"

"Probably," the EMT said as he jotted down notes on a form attached to a clipboard. "But we need to take him to the hospital for x-rays and to have a doctor thoroughly examine him, just to make sure there's nothing going on internally. The impact of the bullet hit pretty close to some vital organs. So, let's get you up into the ambulance and on your way."

Sarah's worry increased, but she bit her bottom lip and remained silent, not wanting her presence to disturb anyone in any way. Levi needed a doctor and she didn't want to distract anyone from that.

He gave the paramedic a perturbed look. "Do I have to go by ambulance?" he asked, casting a quick glance at Sarah.

She felt her face warm at that direct look. Levi obviously hadn't forgotten her presence.

After a lingering moment, Levi shifted his gaze back to the paramedic. "Can't Nick take me to the hospital?"

"No," the EMT replied with a serious shake of his head. "Your blood pressure is a bit high, and while it's probably normal considering what you just went through, I want you monitored until you're under a doctor's care."

"Come on, Kincaid," Nick said in a humorous voice. "Be a big boy and behave."

Levi gave his partner the finger, and Nick just laughed it off.

When Levi stood up and slowly straightened so he could climb into the back of the ambulance, Sarah made a split-second decision, despite how late at night it was. Not to mention how foolish it was to allow herself to get further emotionally involved with this man.

"Can I go with him?" she asked.

The surprise and genuine pleasure that lit up Levi's face when he looked at her was well worth her spontaneous request. Then again, it wasn't as though she had anything or anyone waiting for her back at the motel, so why not spend a few extra hours with the man who'd just saved her life? She justified her rationale, knowing too well her actions weren't motivated by gratitude as much as concern. Once she was certain he hadn't suffered any internal injuries, she would head back to her place and try to forget about Levi Kincaid. *Try* being the operative word.

The EMT shrugged. "Sure, you can come with, as long as the patient doesn't mind."

"Nope, I don't mind at all," Levi said on a soft, sexy drawl that sent crazy swirls of sensual heat spiraling down through her belly. "Besides, I might need someone to hold my hand while the doctor pokes and prods me."

He was such a rogue, but she couldn't stop the smile that touched her lips. Hand-holding she could handle. But she swore that was all Levi Kincaid was getting out of her.

AS SOON AS Levi arrived at the hospital, he was whisked away for a multitude of tests, leaving Sarah to worry and pace out in the waiting room by herself. She wanted to ask for an update, but since she wasn't family, she knew there was no way anyone would release any kind of information to her. Which left her biting her thumbnail as she wore a back-and-forth path through the industrial-strength carpeting.

Nearly an hour later—which seemed like a lifetime—a nurse came out and approached her. "Are you Sarah Robins?"

"Yes," she replied anxiously.

The other woman smiled, obviously used to dealing with nervous visitors. "Levi's tests are complete and he's been assigned a private room."

Sarah exhaled a relieved breath. "So, he's okay?"

"For now, he seems fine," the nurse said, not confirming or denying anything. "The doctor will know more as soon as he has the chance to go over the test results, which should be soon."

"Can I see him?" Sarah asked, unable to stand waiting in the lounge any longer.

The nurse nodded, her eyes sparkling with amusement. "Actually, he sent me out here to get *you*, so follow me and I'll take you to his room."

Sarah trailed behind the woman as they walked past the emergency room triage and down a corridor lined with numbered rooms. The nurse stopped at a door marked with a number eight.

"He's right inside," she said, then turned around and walked back toward the ER.

Sarah pushed the door open and tentatively stepped into the small room, the rubber on the bottom of her tennis shoes letting out a tiny squeak on the linoleum floor. Levi glanced in her direction with an irritable scowl, but as soon as he realized that it was her, an undeniably pleased smile lit up his face, causing her heart to race a bit faster and making her weak in the knees.

From the very first night she'd met him, the man had had that kind of bone-melting effect on her, and it was unlike anything she'd ever experienced. He also made her want to throw caution and common sense to the wind, so *just one time* she could experience being the sole focus of Levi's affection and attention. The sensual thought made her shiver as she moved toward him.

He was sitting up in bed, and she took in the hospital gown he still wore, which left his legs bare from the knees down, and yeah, *she looked*. His calves were nice and toned, *and she couldn't believe she was even thinking this*, but even his *feet* were sexy.

"What was the grumpy look for when I walked in?" she asked as she rounded his bed to the other side. There were two chairs situated there for visitors, but she decided to stand. She didn't intend to stay long. As soon as she was assured he was all right, she planned to leave.

"Oh, you saw that?" he asked with a small smirk. "I thought you were the nurse coming back for more blood tests, and I was hoping to scare her off."

She laughed. "They don't seem easily intimidated around here."

"It was worth a try," he said, then his expression turned serious as he met her gaze. "You stayed," he said, the low, husky tone of his voice stroking along her body like a caress. "I wasn't sure you'd stick around once they admitted me for the tests."

"You took a bullet for me," she pointed out, just in case he'd forgotten that not-so-little detail in tonight's excitement. "I wasn't going to leave without knowing you were okay."

"I appreciate it." He pushed his fingers through his dark blond hair, which only tousled the thick strands even more. As he lowered his hand, his IV tubing got tangled around another cord that tugged at an electrode patch attached to his chest. The wires pulled taut, causing his gown to slip down a few inches, and he released an annoyed growl.

"Hold on." Before his frustration got the better of him, Sarah moved closer and separated the cables so he didn't rip the IV out of his hand or disengage the machine monitoring his pulse and heartbeat. "There you go."

"Thank you," he muttered. "Jesus, I don't know why they need to have me hooked up to all this crap." He settled back against the raised mattress, his expression surly. "They even took *six* vials of my blood," he added, showing her the small bandage on the inside of his arm.

God, he was a terrible patient, and it took effort for Sarah not to laugh at his cranky disposition. "I'm sorry I wasn't here to hold your hand while they stuck that big, bad needle into your arm," she teased.

His grumpiness vanished as a very sly look flitted across his features. "It's not too late to make up for that. You can hold my hand *now*," he dared, and extended his right hand toward her.

There was no doubt in Sarah's mind that he was goading her to touch him—and hand-holding, as innocent as it seemed, would be deliberate and intimate contact between them. Still, she wasn't about to let him win the challenge, and she reached out and settled her hand in his much larger, warmer one. He curled his fingers around hers, capturing her in more ways than one.

He gently skimmed his thumb across her knuckles, the caress making her envision what it would feel like to have that same finger grazing over her taut, sensitive nipple. Which was incredibly stupid of her to even imagine, considering the mere thought made the tips of her breasts tingle and peak against her cotton T-shirt.

Levi's gaze lowered to her chest for a few lingering seconds to enjoy her telling reaction to him, then gradually lifted back up to her face again.

There was no missing the heat building behind his gaze, which matched the one smoldering in her belly. "So, I think you've had more than enough time to think about the question I asked you back at the store before we were rudely interrupted by a robber," he said, injecting humor into his voice. "Are you finally going to say yes to a date and put me out of my misery? And before you answer that, don't forget . . . I did take a bullet to protect you."

The man was utterly shameless, using her gratitude against her, and it took effort for her not to laugh out loud, because despite everything, she found him so damn charming. "Are you seriously going to use the I-took-a-bullet-for-you card and blackmail me?"

"Yes," he replied unrepentantly while trying to hide his own smile. "Are you seriously going to say no again and completely devastate me?"

More than anything, she wanted to give him the answer he desired. Hell, it was what she wanted, too. Everything about Levi Kincaid was intriguing and tempting, and she couldn't remember the last time, if ever, a man had made her feel so desirable and, yes, special. And God, she was so tired of being alone, and lonely, every day except for the time she spent at work.

But she didn't have a great track record when it came to the male gender. She'd been burned badly, twice, because she'd made the mistake of trusting a few jerks she'd thought were good guys. Too many times she'd gotten complacent and let herself be lulled into a false sense of security—starting with her own family, to a specific foster home, to the guys she'd dated—only to end up with broken promises that had chipped away at her heart. It was a repetitive story in her life, and a painful pattern she wanted so badly to break.

If she weren't on the run from a controlling ex-boyfriend, if she didn't have plans to leave town *soon*, it would be so easy to fall for a man like Levi. But unfortunately, that wasn't her reality. But she could accept the date, as long as he understood a few things first.

She shifted on her feet, and without thinking, she ran her tongue across her bottom lip before speaking. He released a low, sexy groan as his gaze zeroed in on her mouth, and the awareness in the small room thickened.

"Are you trying to deliberately tempt me with what I can't have?" The tone of his voice was hungry in a way that had nothing to do with food and everything to do with *her*.

"What?" She tried to make sense of his words, and when his question finally registered—*he wanted her mouth*—she quickly shook her head. "No!" she rushed to say as a warm flush swept across her cheeks. "I wasn't trying to tempt you at all!"

A slow, sensual smile eased across his lips. "Just

for the record, *everything* about you tempts me," he murmured.

There went those weak knees again. Before they could get any more off track with their conversation, Sarah said what was on her mind. "Levi, I need you to know that I'm not looking for anything serious right now."

"Fair enough," he said as his thumb started rubbing softly along the back of the hand he was still holding. "I'm not asking for a lifetime commitment, either. Just a simple, casual night out with you. We can see where it goes from there."

"If I agree to a date, it will be a one-time deal, Levi," she told him as she tried to nonchalantly extricate her hand from his.

He wouldn't let her go and instead grinned confidently. "Then I'll just have to do my damndest to change your mind."

She refrained, just barely, from rolling her eyes at him. The man was persistent to a fault, even a little arrogant, and his determination wasn't worth arguing over. "Okay, fine. Sunday evening you can take me out on a date."

"See?" Triumph deepened his tone. "That wasn't so hard, was it?"

This time, she *did* roll her eyes at him. "You wore down my resistance."

"I knew I would." He winked at her. "If you'll give me your address, I'll pick you up at your place at five p.m."

A flash of panic surged through her when she

thought about him arriving at the seedy, run-down motel where she was staying temporarily. "I'll meet you at the restaurant." She didn't want to deal with the shame and humiliation of having to explain her living situation.

"You agreed to a *date*, not a meet and greet," he said as he gave her hand a squeeze. "I'm picking you up."

God, the man was so stubborn and tenacious, so she gave him the best compromise she'd allow. "Then pick me up at the store. I'll be there by five."

He frowned at her in a way that told Sarah he was analyzing her unusual reaction and was trying to figure out a way around her request, which she refused to allow.

"It's a deal breaker, Levi." Her tone was adamant. "Pick me up at the store or no date. You can't have everything your way."

The corner of his mouth twitched with humor, but he finally relented. "Fine. You win. *This* time."

Loud male voices drifted into the room from the corridor outside, and Sarah watched as a sudden look of irritation passed across his features.

"Shit," he muttered beneath his breath.

She had no idea what had caused the change in his demeanor. "What's wrong?"

The line of his jaw tensed. "You'll see in three . . . two . . . one—"

Sarah literally jumped when two big, good-looking men unexpectedly barged into the room, the older-looking one of the two speaking as they advanced toward Levi's hospital bed.

"Jesus Christ, Levi!" the guy bellowed angrily. "You were fucking shot and you didn't think to call one of your brothers to let us know?"

Oh, God, his brothers, and here she was, holding Levi's hand like she was his girlfriend or someone he was intimately involved with. She tugged her fingers out of his grasp, hard enough that he was forced to let her go, but the other man with sleeves of tattoos wrapping around both muscled arms noticed—and smirked.

"Calm down, Clay," Levi said, back to being grumpy. He glared at both brothers as they stopped on the other side of his bed. "The bullet hit my vest and it wasn't life threatening. I'm just here for some routine testing before they'll release me."

The man named Clay glanced at Sarah, and there was no denying the quick spark of curiosity in his gaze before he pinned his brother with a direct and concerned look. "Well, *your partner* thought it was important enough to call us."

That bit of information seemed to annoy Levi even more. He clearly didn't like being coddled by anyone. "I have a fractured rib, but other than that, *I'm fine*," he insisted, even though the doctor had yet to come into the room to go over his test results. "Or at least I was until you two came charging in here."

The tattooed guy—who looked like a total bad boy who wasn't the least bit put off by Levi's gruff demeanor—merely grinned at his brother. "Yeah, sorry to interrupt . . . whatever we interrupted," he said, not sounding the least bit contrite.

In fact, Sarah was certain he was deliberately goading Levi, and she found herself suddenly fascinated by the three brothers who clearly had very different dispositions.

The bad-boy brother took in Levi's hospital gown and bare legs, that provoking smirk reappearing. "Nice dress, by the way," he teased. "Though next time, you might want to shave your legs."

Levi narrowed his gaze at his brother. "Don't be a dick, Mason." There was a distinct warning note in his voice, but Mason only seemed amused by Levi's threatening tone.

"Knock it off, Mason," Clay said, obviously the peace-keeper in the family, before settling his frown back on Levi. "I'm glad you're okay, but you still should have called us. I nearly had a heart attack when Nick's first words were, 'Levi's been shot,' before he clarified that you were wearing your bulletproof vest."

"Got it," Levi said, finally relenting. "Won't happen again."

"So, are you going to introduce us to your . . .?" Mason let the sentence trail off, waiting for either Levi or Sarah to fill in the missing word.

"Friend," she said quickly, and since they were on opposite sides of Levi's bed, she gave both brothers a friendly wave. "I'm Sarah, and Levi was at the convenience store where I work when I was held up by an armed robber. I'm here just to make sure that he's truly okay before I head home."

Clay's gaze was filled with understanding, but Mason's glance was much more inquisitive, and it was that small smile on his face that made her wonder what, exactly, he was thinking. Thankfully, neither one of them asked her any other questions. Instead, Clay returned his attention to Levi and insisted on knowing the details of what happened.

While Levi gave them the quick version of their night, it gave Sarah a few extra minutes to really compare the three brothers. Clay's and Mason's hair was much darker than Levi's lighter brown, and while Levi had green eyes, both his brothers' were blue. Clay and Mason *looked* like brothers, with similar facial features, but she never would have guessed that Levi was their sibling.

Then there were their individual personality traits, she thought, as she watched each brother deal with Levi in distinctly different ways. Clay was protective, almost parental in his concern. Mason, well, he didn't seem too serious about anything, though she had seen the initial worry on his face when he'd walked into the room. But now, he was all about giving his brother a hard time, which Sarah found endearing, even if it annoyed the hell out of Levi.

She wondered where Levi's parents were and figured they probably lived farther away and Clay would give them an update on Levi's condition. Or maybe they'd passed away, she thought with a pang of sadness that crept up on her before she could stop it.

Despite the absence of any parents, she could see and feel the connection between these brothers, and it made her all too aware of her *lack* of family. Levi had people who obviously cared a lot about him, and she envied that close-knit bond that they shared. One she'd lost when she was eight years old. Her whole entire family gone in one fell swoop that had left her devastated, lost, and completely alone. And while she might have gotten past the emotional devastation, she was *still* lost and alone.

The doctor finally arrived, and as soon as the older man walked into the room, the three brothers all grew quiet, each one of them looking at the physician expectantly as he stopped beside Levi's bed.

"Hello, Mr. Kincaid. I'm Dr. Fisher. I finally had the chance to look over your CT scan, x-rays, and blood test results," he said as he swiped a finger across the screen of the tablet he was carrying, his gaze reading whatever he'd pulled up on the small computer. "It appears that you have two fractured ribs on your lower left side, but your liver and kidneys are functioning fine, and you were spared any internal damage. Your lungs look good, as well."

Sarah exhaled in gratitude and relief.

"Thank God," Clay said beneath his breath, the worry furrowing his brows easing a bit.

"Damn, you're like Superman," Mason said in awe.

"Ironman, according to Nick," Levi corrected his brother.

"All in all, you're going to be fine," the doctor

went on. "It's going to take a good month for your ribs to heal completely. In about two to three weeks, you can return to work on light duty until your personal physician releases you to full duty. In the meantime, you need to rest, take it easy, and don't do anything strenuous. You'll have severe bruising in that area, and I can give you a prescription for Vicodin or Norco to control the pain—"

"I don't want any painkillers," Levi said, abruptly cutting off the doctor.

Dr. Fisher blinked at him in surprise, and even Sarah was taken aback by the harsh tone of his voice. The only ones who didn't seem concerned about Levi's adamant refusal were Clay and Mason, which she found interesting. Clearly, Levi had an issue with those types of narcotics, and she couldn't deny that she was curious as to why.

"You might need them to be comfortable, at least for a few days," the doctor said, trying again.

Levi shook his head, his expression resolute. "I don't want them. I'll be fine. If I'm uncomfortable, I'll take ibuprofen."

"Okay," the doctor relented. "If you change your mind, just call my office. I'll make sure the nurse gives you my number when she brings in your discharge papers. Once that's done, you're free to leave."

"Thanks, Doc," Levi said.

Once the man was gone, Sarah decided it was time for her to go, too. She didn't need to stick around while Levi was unhooked from the monitor and IV and got dressed. His brothers could help him in any way he might need.

"Now that I know that you really are fine, I'm going to head home," she said, smiling when Levi glanced at her with those warm green eyes.

"How?" he asked.

She tipped her head in confusion at his odd question. "How what?"

"How are you going to get home when you rode in the ambulance here?"

Oh, yeah, that. She really loved that he was so concerned, when the guys who'd passed through her life so far wouldn't have thought twice about her safety. She had every intention of calling a cab since the buses weren't running this late at night—or morning, as the case might be—but instinctively knew that Levi wouldn't stand for that.

"If you need a ride, we can take you home," Clay said, his concern for her equally genuine.

Sarah swallowed past the unexpected gratitude tightening in her throat—along with the urge to say, *yes, please*, but there was no way she wanted any of these men to see how and where she lived. "I appreciate the offer, but I have a friend who's waiting for me to call her to come and pick me up," she lied, ignoring the way that Levi scrutinized her—as if he could see right through her fib, which she hoped wasn't the case. She needed to get out of there before he figured out the truth.

"Take it easy, Levi." She gave his arm a friendly

squeeze, and though she didn't mention their date on Sunday, she knew there was no way he'd forget—she could see it in his eyes.

She walked around the bed and glanced at Clay, then Mason. "It was nice meeting you both."

"Same here," Clay said, then nodded toward Mason. "And I hope this knucklehead didn't give the two of us a bad first impression."

Said *knucklehead* merely flashed her a charming grin, and she laughed. "No, not at all." She'd enjoyed watching the three siblings interact.

"Good." Clay gave her a warm smile. "I hope we see each other again, hopefully under much more pleasant circumstances next time."

She doubted it. "Me, too," she said politely, though she wasn't going to be around long enough to have anything more to do with this close-knit family. The thought made her sad, and she rushed out the door before the ever-perceptive Levi could call her on the emotions she knew were shining in her eyes.

Chapter Three

FOUR LONG DAYS of lying around and resting, and Levi was bored out of his mind. He'd been released from active duty for at least the next two weeks, and because he couldn't exert himself just yet, he couldn't even work on the projects around the house that he enjoyed doing on his days off. So, instead, he'd binge-watched movies and television series on Netflix. He was now caught up on all the latest episodes of his favorite shows and had a deeper understanding of the phrase *couch potato*.

Since the shooting on Tuesday, he'd had a visitor every day. Wednesday, Nick and a couple of other guys from the station had come over to hang out for a few hours. Thursday, Clay stopped by in the afternoon to make sure he was feeling better. He'd brought a pizza and stayed to watch a few episodes of a show with him, and on Friday, Mason dropped by for the sole purpose of being a general pain in the ass. And of course, to pry about his relationship with Sarah, about which Levi gave his brother nothing to satisfy his burning curiosity.

By Saturday, all Levi wanted was peace and quiet and no more visitors. Well, that wasn't completely true. He wouldn't have turned away Sarah if she'd knocked on his door. But she didn't know where he lived, and they hadn't exchanged phone numbers for her to call or text. He could have driven over to Circle K during one of her night shifts—and he'd seriously thought about it—but the last thing he wanted her to think was that he was stalking her, even if he was a cop. He just had to trust that she'd be at the store tomorrow evening at the specified time for him to pick her up for their date.

And what was up with Sarah being so stubborn about that particular request, anyway? Levi wondered with a frown as he channel-surfed for something to hold his attention on TV. Of course he'd agreed to her terms, but her insistence had only piqued his curiosity and made him determined to find out why she was being so evasive. Just like she'd refused Clay's offer to drive her home the night at the hospital, which would have been much easier and more convenient than bothering a friend.

There was so much about Sarah that was a mystery, and granted, that was part of her allure. She was a puzzle to him, an enigma that made him want to know more about her. And that, in itself, was a novelty for him when it came to women. He really wanted to strip away those guarded layers of hers to discover all the secrets he instinctively knew she was keeping from him.

He didn't miss the irony of that thought process. He, himself, certainly wasn't a stranger to holding on to his fair share of secrets. His were dark and nightmarish, thanks to a hellish, violent childhood that had shaped the frightened boy he'd been and had also provided the catalyst for the man he'd become. One who valued control in all aspects of his life, including masking his emotions and rarely letting anyone close. Especially women. Which was why his fascination with Sarah was so damn out of character for him . . . yet it was that same unexplainable fascination that had him pursuing her.

After flipping through a few more channels, he finally settled on reruns of an old sitcom, but halfway into the show, the doorbell rang. He groaned and dropped his head back against the couch. He *really* wasn't in the mood for company, but he couldn't ignore the person at the door. His truck was in the driveway, so clearly he was inside. If he'd been smart, he would have parked it in the garage to give the appearance of nobody being home.

Another irritating *ding-dong, ding-dong*, followed by a firm knock. He swore beneath his breath and moved off the sofa too quickly. A sharp, stabbing pain in his side made him wince, and he pressed his hand to the still-sore spot against his rib cage. *Great*, he thought irritably, knowing that he'd be dealing with a nagging throb for the next half hour.

Since he hadn't been expecting any visitors, he was wearing an old, comfortable pair of sweat pants and a faded T-shirt. His feet were bare, he'd only finger combed his hair this morning after getting up, and he had a layer of scruff on his face since he hadn't bothered to shave. At least he'd brushed his teeth.

He reached the door just as another knock sounded, and he frowned when he looked through the peephole and saw *three* female faces on the other side. What the hell were *they* doing here? he wondered, though his gut told him that Clay and Mason had sent the trio over to check on him—or torment him. He wasn't sure which, but what he did know was that his brothers were assholes for sending *these* three women to his place, especially when he'd made it clear he wanted to be left alone today.

"We know you're in there, so open up and let us in." This from bold and sassy Katrina, who was Mason's fiancée and the only woman who'd been able to tame Mason's wild man-whore ways. Next month, the two of them were getting married.

"We already saw you looking through the peephole, Levi," Tara added—who was the main bartender at Kincaid's and now manager of the place since Clay had gotten married. "The gig is up."

"I have Clay's key and I'm not afraid to use it," came a sugar-sweet threat from Samantha, Clay's wife and the best thing that had ever happened to Levi's older brother.

Knowing he was outnumbered, he finally opened the door. "Did you ladies not get the memo? No visitors allowed today."

"Then it's a good thing we're family and not visitors," Samantha said with a pretty smile as she lifted the large plate she was holding so he could see the contents through the plastic wrap. "I brought you my caramel fleur de sel French macaroons."

Damn. His mouth immediately watered. Samantha was a phenomenal pastry chef, and her macaroons were *amazing.* Those little delights were a bribe he couldn't resist.

"*You* may enter." He stepped back so Samantha could walk inside, then blocked the way again, his gaze taking in the glass dish covered in foil that Katrina was carrying. "What do you have?"

Katrina, with her purple-tipped blonde hair and an arm covered in colorful butterfly tattoos, flashed him a knowing grin. "Chicken enchiladas, extra cheese."

His favorite, of course, and on cue, his stomach growled hungrily. He glanced at Tara, and she automatically lifted a gallon jug of orange juice as her offering, which was his drink of choice.

"You ladies do *not* play fair," he grumbled good-naturedly as he let Katrina and Tara into the house, as well.

"Every man has a weakness, and we just happen to know yours," Katrina said as she passed by.

The delicious scent of Mexican food teased his senses, and he followed the girls into his kitchen, realizing just how ravenous he was. He hadn't eaten anything since having a late breakfast, which had only been a bowl of cereal, and he was suddenly grateful that they'd brought food with them.

Samantha set her plate on the counter and shooed him toward the adjoining living room. "You're supposed to be resting. Go and make yourself comfortable on the couch, and we'll bring the enchiladas to you."

He wanted to argue that *he was fine*, that despite the occasional pain from the fractured ribs, he was more than capable of taking care of himself, and he could certainly serve up his own plate. He'd been fending for himself since he was a kid under far more traumatic circumstances, but his sister-in-law was giving him a firm look that clearly stated she was now in charge, and he did what any intelligent man would do. He went and settled himself on the couch, with his legs up on the ottoman, and waited for dinner to come to him.

He didn't have to wait long. Ten minutes later, the trio came out of the kitchen, each of them carrying something different. Katrina gave him the plate with the steaming chicken enchiladas, and Tara set a tall glass of orange juice on the side table so it was within reach. Samantha placed the pastries on the coffee table for later, then settled on the sofa next to him, with the other two girls sitting around him, as well.

As he took a bite of the soft corn tortillas stuffed with savory goodness, he had to admit that having three women fussing over him wasn't half bad. But it also made him all too aware of the fact that Clay and Mason were lucky enough to have Samantha and Katrina in their lives *every day*, as their best friends and partners in all things, and he was suddenly the odd man out and feeling more alone than ever.

He was truly happy for both of his siblings, but he'd definitely noticed a shift in their relationship now that Clay was married and Mason was engaged. He saw his brothers less often and didn't talk to them as much as before. They were living their new lives, just as they should . . . while he was living the same day-to-day existence. A life that was routine and predictable and safe, just how he liked it.

He'd always been a loner, and he definitely enjoyed women, but he'd never met one that made him want to share *everything* with her, including his past, the present, and the future. Because of all the shit he'd been through in his life, that was too much of a vulnerable place for him to venture. Ever. He had too many jagged, broken pieces inside of him, and he couldn't imagine any woman in her right mind who would take a chance on a lifetime commitment to someone so irreparably damaged. Even if somehow his brothers had managed to find special women, Levi didn't see the same happy ending for himself.

While he ate his dinner, the girls asked him questions about the shooting, and because they'd arrived at his place with the best kind of gifts, he regaled them with all the details, until they were all staring at him wide-eyed and in awe. And then they finally got down to the *real* reason they'd stopped by. To interrogate him about the mysterious woman whom Clay and Mason had met but Levi had remained tight-lipped about.

"So, tell us about Sarah, the girl you saved," Samantha said, her blue eyes filled with curiosity.

Saved was a little dramatic when he'd just been doing his job. "What about her?" Levi responded, being deliberately vague as he finished the last bite of his dinner, then set the plate on the side table.

"Clay said that she was in your hospital room when he got there with Mason," Samantha explained as she tucked her legs beneath her on the couch.

"She was," he replied, and gave her the most logical explanation. "She wanted to make sure I was okay and rode over to the hospital with me in the ambulance."

"Wow, that's kind of romantic," Tara said, and while she was the most level-headed of the three, he didn't miss the teasing glimmer in her gaze that told him she was totally yanking his chain. Such a smartass.

"It really wasn't a big deal." He took a drink of his orange juice, praying that the conversation about Sarah ended. Like, now.

"Mason told me that when he walked in, you were holding her hand, but she was quick to pull hers away," Katrina said, and Levi nearly choked on his juice. "He said she had that whole caught-in-the-act look in her eyes, like she was hiding something . . . like the two of you being together."

His brother was such a big-mouthed fucker, and now Levi was 99.9% sure that Mason had encouraged Katrina, probably along with Samantha and Tara, to come over to find out the nitty-gritty details.

Mason was constantly giving Levi shit about his *lack* of female companionship, but getting laid, when he *wanted* to, wasn't an issue for Levi. He was just more discriminate about his extracurricular activities and didn't broadcast or flaunt his affairs. He always kept them private, therefore Mason thought he was celibate, and compared to his brother's past exploits— before he'd settled down with Katrina—Levi supposed he *was* like a monk.

Samantha picked up the plate with the macaroons and handed them to Levi, and just as he was close to putting one in his mouth, she ruined the moment by asking, "*Are* you two dating?"

Goddamn, he *really* wanted to indulge in one of the light, airy, crème-filled cookies, to have a quiet moment to savor the salted caramel and almond pastry as it melted in his mouth. But all their personal questions were making it impossible for him to enjoy himself.

Placing the macaroon on top of the others, he put the dessert aside for later, then looked at the trio, who were all waiting anxiously for his answer. "I'm sorry to disappoint all three of you, but no, we're not dating." It wasn't a lie. They weren't going on an official date until tomorrow night.

"Oh," Samantha said in quiet disappointment. "We were just kind of hoping . . ."

Levi scrubbed a frustrated hand along the stubble on his jaw and narrowed his gaze at his sister-in-law. She couldn't just say something like that and leave him hanging. "You were hoping *what*?"

"That maybe the two of you were an item and we'd get to meet her," Tara said, answering before Samantha could.

Seriously? Wasn't going to happen. In fact, under normal circumstances, Sarah probably never would have met his brothers. That's just the way it was for him.

Katrina gave him a pointed look. "You know, in the twelve years that I've known you, I've never even heard you mention a girlfriend, let alone met one of them." A small amused smile eased across her lips. "Mason swears you're still a virgin. Or gay."

Levi literally gaped at her. *Un-fucking-believable.* His brother was such a wise ass. "Well, you can assure him that I'm definitely *not* gay, and I haven't been a virgin since my senior year in high school." *And what the hell—was he really defending his sex life to the three women who were like sisters to him?*

"Really?" Katrina's brows rose in surprise. "In high school, you were so. . ."

Withdrawn. Introverted. An outsider. As a moody, hormonal teenager with a shit-ton of family issues, being stand-offish had been his only way to maintain control of his emotions. Except there had been an equally moody Goth girl who'd followed him into the bathroom one day while everyone else was in class, pushed him up against the wall, put her hand on his dick, and said, *I want you to fuck me.*

It was an offer his cock couldn't refuse, and even that first time, he'd recognized his need to be the one in control, and those dominant urges had only increased every time they screwed around. There had been nothing emotional about their encounters. They didn't talk about their lives or share personal things with each other. Hell, he'd only known her name because she'd been in one of his classes. And because their trysts were all about a physical release, she'd let him fuck her however he wanted, however he needed—rough, aggressive, demanding, with her on her knees, or her hands restrained, and him in charge.

Yeah, he'd picked up on his needs early in life. The situation had worked for the both of them, and after graduation they'd gone their separate ways. And by then, his sexual preferences had been set.

Levi shook his head of the memory, unable to believe how off track the entire discussion about Sarah had gone and where his thoughts had traveled. He glanced at all three women, desperate to put an end to the subject. "I'm not having this conversation with you guys."

Samantha reached out and gently squeezed his arm, her gaze soft and warm and nurturing. "We just want you to be happy."

He softened at the heartfelt statement, appreciating the fact that they cared. "I'm perfectly happy," he said, even as he realized he'd just contradicted his earlier thoughts about feeling left out and alone now that his brothers were in committed relationships. But being on his own worked for him. The women he was with might enjoy that darker, more dominant side to his personality when it came to sex, but emotionally, he had nothing to offer long term.

He exhaled a deep breath, suddenly feeling tired and worn out. "Look, Sarah is a friend. Can we leave it at that?"

Thankfully, all three girls agreed to let it go for now, but he had a feeling that their interest in Sarah wasn't over. Not by a long shot.

SARAH GLANCED OUT the glass window from the inside of Circle K as she waited anxiously for a certain hot, gorgeous guy to pick her up for their date. She would have stood outside, but when she'd arrived a few minutes ago, there had been three sketchy-looking guys loitering by the side of the building, and after being held up just a few days ago, she found herself much more suspicious of the people in the area. She felt safer hanging inside with the two cashiers who were working the Sunday night shift.

She had no idea what kind of car Levi drove, but figured he'd pull up to the mart and see her standing inside. As minutes passed, she grew more anxious—a combination of nerves and anticipation swirling like a dozen butterflies set free in her stomach. It had been a long time since she'd been on a date with a man. Even with Dylan, he'd never taken her out somewhere nice with romantic intentions, and once they'd arrived at Sacrosanct, she'd been locked inside the compound, and her life for those three weeks had changed drastically, until she'd finally escaped.

She still wasn't sure if it had been a smart idea to say yes to Levi, but she'd told herself a dozen times that *one* evening with him wouldn't hurt. She'd been living a lonely, solitary life the past five weeks—being holed up in her shitty motel room during the day and venturing out in the evenings to work. Was it so wrong of her to want to enjoy a night of easy conversation with Levi, along with the flirting and the attraction that made her feel sexy and desired?

She'd already made it clear that this date was a one-time deal, and she intended to stand by that claim. She'd also decided that at some point tonight she was going to tell Levi that she was leaving Chicago, probably within the next few weeks, and a statement like that was certain to put a damper on his future interest in her. And that, she told herself, was for the best.

She watched as a white, sporty four-door pickup turned into the lot and headed toward the store. As the vehicle neared, she clearly saw Levi through the windshield. Her heart began to race in her chest, and she suddenly felt like she was back in high school. And along with that thought came those same self-conscious feelings about what she was wearing.

Living in foster homes for the better part of her young life, most of her clothes had been second-hand—faded, worn, and always out of style. She'd never had pretty outfits, and even though she was currently on a strict budget, she'd splurged at Walmart and had bought a cute and flirty royal blue tank dress off the clearance rack for nine bucks. She'd found a pair of black, patent-leather-looking flip-flops—i.e., *plastic*—that had been stylish but only a few dollars. And even though she desperately needed the ends of her hair trimmed, she left it down instead of up in its normal ponytail. At least it was shiny and soft to the touch. But her outfit was still cheap, and she felt awkward as she waited for him to park.

As soon as he pulled in, she went outside to meet him, a huge smile on her lips despite her insecurities. He turned off the engine and immediately got out of the truck, and when he started toward her, she noticed the intense scowl on his handsome face. Before she could greet Levi, and without a single word from him, he took her arm in his firm grasp and escorted her to the passenger side of the vehicle. He opened the door and helped her up onto the seat. As she buckled her safety belt, he hand-locked her door before closing it, then rounded the pickup to the driver's side.

Once he was settled in his own seat, he glanced at her, still wearing that fierce expression, and she had no idea why. "Is something wrong?" she asked tentatively.

"Yeah, there is," he said as a muscle in his jaw twitched. "Can I just say that I fucking *hate* that you work here?"

Startled at the unexpected vehemence in his tone,

she stared at him with wide eyes, not sure what to say to that.

"You've already been accosted by a robber, this is a crappy neighborhood, and I'm pretty sure those three guys over there are up to no good," he went on gruffly, his gaze flicking to the men who had prompted her to wait inside the mart earlier. "Then you come walking out of that store looking so goddamn sweet in that dress, and all three of those assholes turned to leer at you. I'm pretty sure if I hadn't made it fucking clear that you were with me, they would have been all over you."

"I'm sorry," she said, meaning it. She might have no alternative, but she was grateful he cared enough to be upset.

He exhaled a harsh breath that seemed to calm him a bit. "Thinking about you working here at night gives me a goddamn ulcer," he muttered as he shoved his fingers through his hair. "I. Fucking. *Hate it.*"

She hated it, too. So much, and even more after being held up with a gun pointed at her head. She'd even started having little anxiety attacks when certain people walked into the store, and she honestly couldn't wait to have enough money saved so she could quit and move on.

"It's only temporary, until . . ." The words came out before she could think them through. She cut them off, but she definitely caught his attention.

"Until what?" he asked with a frown. "Do you have another job lined up somewhere?"

"Sort of," she hedged, not sure she wanted to *start* their date with the depressing news of her impending departure from Chicago.

He narrowed his gaze. "What does 'sort of' mean?"

"I'm leaving town in a few weeks," she said, getting it all out in the open.

He studied her face too intently. "Why?"

"Personal reasons." She tried not to squirm under his intense scrutiny and wondered if this was how a suspect felt while being cross-examined by *Officer Kincaid*. It was damn intimidating, but the last thing she wanted to do was drag him into her problems.

She waited for him to push for a better explanation, but after a long stretch of tense silence, he surprised her by backing off.

"Okay," he said much too easily when she could see a dozen more questions still lingering in his gaze.

He started up the truck and turned back onto the street. Hating how quiet it had become between them, she tried to get things back to normal, or else it was going to be a long, awkward night.

"How are you doing and feeling?" She'd thought about him every single day, wondering if the pain had lessened, especially since he'd refused any narcotic medication.

"I'm still sore, but managing," he said, his tone back to the Levi she knew—not the interrogating cop.

She took in his strong profile as he drove. Her gaze settled on his full lips, and she couldn't help but wonder what it would feel like to kiss him. It certainly wasn't the first time she'd had that thought, and she'd already decided that if he made the attempt tonight, she'd let him. If there was only one thing she could take with her when she left town, it would be knowing what Levi tasted like. She imagined the flavor of heat and all-consuming passion.

She felt a little pulse between her legs, and she folded her hands in her lap and rerouted her too sensual thoughts. "When do you go back to work?"

"Hopefully in a few weeks." He turned his head, and this time there was a genuine smile on his lips. "My family is driving me crazy."

She laughed, because she'd already met his brothers and could only imagine how boisterous the rest of his family was. "Lots of visitors coming by?"

He groaned. "You have no idea. I've put a permanent ban on anyone stopping by without calling first."

"How did your parents take the news of you getting shot?" she asked curiously.

He visibly stiffened, and his hands tightened on the steering wheel. "My parents have been gone a long time," he said abruptly. "It's just me and my brothers."

She didn't miss the thread of bitterness in his voice, which struck her as odd, considering she knew how difficult it was to lose your parents and family members. But judging by his closed-off body language, he didn't seem to want to discuss the issue further, so she wasn't about to pry. Instead, she gave him the moment he seemed to need to gather his composure again.

After a few minutes passed, he exhaled a deep breath. "So, how does Italian sound for dinner?" he asked.

"Amazing," she said, almost too eagerly. After living on ramen and bland meals for weeks, the thought of something so savory had her stomach growling in anticipation. "Where are we going?"

He glanced over at her and grinned. "My place."

Chapter Four

L EVI WAS TAKING her to his place. Sarah had mixed emotions about his announcement, because that meant they were going to be completely alone, instead of surrounded by people in a restaurant. Then again, this meant she had him all to herself for the night, and that made her . . . incredibly happy.

His two-story house was located on the outskirts of Chicago in what looked like a family-friendly neighborhood. On a late Sunday afternoon, kids were outside playing while adults were washing their cars, doing yard work, or sitting on their porch to enjoy the warm day. Levi waved to his neighbor as he turned into a driveway, then pulled the truck into the garage.

Once inside the house, she followed him into the kitchen. The decor was masculine, and from what she could see of the living room, there was a large brown sofa and ottoman, and a ridiculously large TV mounted on the wall. The kitchen itself was nicely laid out with upgraded appliances, and as soon as they entered, Levi set his keys on the counter, then turned around and started toward her.

The sudden sensual hunger shining in his eyes stole her breath as he closed the short distance between them, and when he reached her, he settled his hands on her waist and gently pushed her back, step by step, until she was trapped against the stainless steel refrigerator. The cool metal against her back was a startling contrast to the heat emanating off of him, even though he'd yet to press his body against hers. And dear Lord, she wanted that. She craved the feel of him—every single inch. Badly.

He let go of her waist and cradled her face in his warm palms. He tipped her head back slightly, so her gaze met his, and she felt herself getting lost in those incredible eyes. The light green irises were mesmerizing. Gorgeous and hypnotic. She could stare into them forever. There was something in the depths as he looked down at her, something that made her feel safe. Made her want to trust him with all her secret hopes and desires.

She couldn't miss the carnal need there, either. She'd never known lust before—had never experienced it and had definitely never seen it etched across a man's features and directed at *her. Two firsts tonight.* Her limbs grew heavy with desire as the hottest, sexiest man she'd ever met stared at her mouth like he was ten seconds away from ravishing her. Excitement and anticipation swirled inside of her belly, and she hoped she didn't have to wait much longer than that.

"First things first," he murmured huskily as he skimmed the pad of his thumb along her lower lip, making them part as if on silent command. "If I don't *finally* feel your mouth against mine, I'm not going to be able to think of anything else during dinner. So, to eliminate that distraction, I need to kiss you. Are you okay with that?"

Unable to form a coherent answer that didn't sound like a whimper of need, she nodded her head. *Oh, yes, please.*

With a slow, sinful smile that made her insides liquefy, his head slowly descended toward hers, and she closed her eyes, wanting to make sure she memorized everything about Levi and this magical, seductive kiss. His lips brushed across hers, so tempting and teasing, and there was nothing she could do to stop the soft sigh that escaped her.

Needing more, she gave in to the urge to slip her tongue out to touch his bottom lip. A low growl rumbled up from his chest, and what had started as slow and sweet suddenly turned hot and wild. With his big hands still framing her face, his mouth took control, opening wide as he slanted his lips firmly against hers while his tongue swept deep inside, making her moan with delight.

The incredibly erotic taste of him filled her senses, and his woodsy, masculine scent wrapped around her like an addictive drug she knew she'd never get enough of. So she took as much as she could *now*, letting him kiss her as hard and deep as he wanted, and quickly learned that he wasn't a man who did anything half-way. The pleasure was indescribable. Beyond decadent and arousing. The intensity was off the charts, and the way he consumed her, the way he claimed her mouth as if he owned it, was nothing short of intoxicating.

She had no idea how much time passed before he finally ended the kiss, but she silently mourned the loss of his lips as they left hers. She opened her eyes, realizing that only two parts of his body had touched her the entire time. His mouth and his hands on her face, when she'd fully expected, and *wanted*, to feel his hard, muscled frame pinning her to the refrigerator. The fact that he hadn't taken advantage of the situation was testament to this man's impressive restraint.

"*Fuck*," he breathed, his expression as dazed as she felt.

She managed a small laugh. "Yeah, that was so worth waiting for."

"*You* were worth waiting for." He glided his thumbs along her cheeks, which felt warm and flushed from his kiss. "By the way, you look beautiful to-night."

Sarah knew she wasn't a classic beauty, but the sincere compliment, combined with the adoring look in his eyes, made her believe it. If only for tonight. "Thank you."

"I have a bottle of wine in the refrigerator," he said with a smile, and to her disappointment, he let her go. "Would you like a glass while I make dinner?"

Ahhh, wine. Another luxury that she wasn't about to refuse. "That sounds great."

She moved away so he could retrieve the Chardonnay from the refrigerator, and she admired his backside—mainly his tight ass as he bent low to retrieve the bottle from the bottom shelf—in his soft, worn jeans. "What's on the menu?"

"Chicken carbonara," he said as he brought down a regular glass from the cupboard before giving her a pointed look. "Do *not* tell me you're one of those women who only eats salad."

She laughed. "Oh, my God, no. I love pasta."

"Good." Seemingly satisfied with her answer, he poured Chardonnay halfway into the tall glass, then brought it to her. "Sorry I don't have wine glasses."

"This will work just fine." She took a drink of the cool, crisp, delicious liquid, watching as he recorked the bottle and put it back into the cooler. "You're not having any?"

He shook his head as he started retrieving various ingredients from the refrigerator to make dinner and set them near the stove. "No. I don't drink."

She didn't want to get in his way while he prepped and cooked the food, so she leaned against the granite counter on the other side of the stove from where he was working. "Wine, or alcohol in general?" she asked curiously as he pulled pots and pans from a cupboard and set them on the glass top burners.

"*Any* alcohol."

He sounded so matter-of-fact about it, but as he'd

also refused a prescription for narcotics, she suspected there was a whole lot more he wasn't revealing when it came to liquor and medications. "Is there a reason why not?" she asked, genuinely wanting to know more. "Do you not like the taste, or did you have a really bad hangover that made you swear off of it altogether?" she teased.

He stopped what he was doing for a moment to glance at her, and there was something painful in his eyes that told her this was an emotional issue for him. "I've never had alcohol," he admitted, his tone deceptively even. "But I saw enough as a kid with both alcohol and drugs to know they're not something I'd like or enjoy. I know they hinder a person's ability to think straight or logically, or function normally, and that lack of control is totally not my thing."

She couldn't help but wonder what he'd seen as a child that made him take such extreme steps as a man. Not to mention, there was that subtle issue with control again. Not in an abusive or aggressive way, but he'd just made it clear that it was important to him to always exercise restraint emotionally, mentally, and physically.

Why—on a deeper level than his pat explanation—was the question, and she found that part of his personality extremely fascinating. "Is that the reason you wouldn't take the prescription for the painkillers from the doctor?"

"Yes."

He gave her nothing more, so she let the subject

go. After all, she had secrets of her own. She drank her wine, a little more self-conscious drinking it now that he chose not to, and watched as he chopped up the pancetta, then sautéed it with garlic and olive oil before adding the chicken to the pan to sear. He had one of those quick-boil burners that had a large pot of water roiling in no time flat. In went the pasta, and while that cooked, he whisked together the ingredients for the cream sauce. He didn't use a recipe, and she was definitely in awe of his chef skills.

"Where did you learn to cook like this?" she asked as he combined everything into one pan and stirred so the sauce coated all the spaghetti.

"Cooking channels and recipes on the Internet," he said with a shrug. "When you grow up eating macaroni and cheese from a box and peanut butter and jelly sandwiches, then go on to eat tasteless MRE packs in the military, your adult palate craves food with more appetizing flavors."

He'd just given her more bits and pieces of his past, and she stored the information away. "I'm so impressed."

He grated a fresh block of parmesan cheese over the pasta dish, then took a fork and twirled the spaghetti and other creamy goodness around the tines. "Taste," he said, and brought it up to her mouth.

She let him feed her the bite, and it was beyond amazing. Her deprived taste buds rejoiced, and she was pretty sure her eyes had just rolled back into her head. "Oh, my God," she moaned. "I need to marry you."

As soon as the words came out—which were meant to be playful and flirty—her eyes widened, and he merely grinned.

"That's kind of hard to do when you're leaving town," he teased right back, but she saw the disappointment and questions in his eyes.

Still, he didn't ask, respecting her privacy as she'd respected his.

He served up two plates, then picked up their dishes from the counter. "Come on, let's go eat."

She followed him over to a small dining table with four chairs. After she sat down, he placed her dinner in front of her, then took a seat across the table. They ate for a few quiet minutes, and she savored and enjoyed every single bite.

"So, what's your story, Sarah Robins?" he asked after a while, his gaze inquisitive.

He was leaving it up to her to tell him only what she wanted. They were both so cautious and wary when it came to sharing anything personal, but she felt comfortable with Levi, in a way that allowed her to trust him with parts of her past. Even the difficult, painful parts. And she'd be a liar if she didn't admit that she hoped if she divulged some things, he'd do the same.

"Well, I grew up in Barrington here in Chicago, and up until the age of eight, I had a great childhood," she said with a smile, because those memories as a happy, carefree kid were the best ones she had.

"Unfortunately, then I lost my parents, my younger brother, and my grandmother in a house fire that was started by an electrical shortage in the living room. From what I was told, the fire spread quickly at the bottom level, and by the time it reached the second story, where all the bedrooms were, the entire house was engulfed in flames, and there was no getting out."

"Holy shit." His forkful of pasta halted right above his plate, and he stared at her incredulously. "You were the only one to get out safely?"

"No, I wasn't home that night." The familiar sadness and guilt tightened in her chest, along with the devastation of having everything familiar and comforting ripped away from her in one fell swoop. "I was at a sleepover at a friend's house. I didn't find out until the next morning, when my friend's mother told me. One day my family was there, and the next, they were gone."

"Damn," he muttered beneath his breath, his gaze soft with sympathy. "I'm so sorry."

"I didn't have any other relatives to live with, so I was put into foster care pretty quickly," she went on, remembering how petrified she'd been like it had happened yesterday instead of so many years ago. "That was scary for a kid who'd just lost her family," she admitted.

"I can only imagine." He ate another bite of his dinner, and it was clear he wanted to know more. "Were you at least placed with a good family?"

She took a drink of wine to give herself a few extra

moments. She'd never told *anyone* this story before, because it was the impetus for so many of the insecurities she carried with her, even as an adult—of not being good enough or loved enough for someone to stay with her, love her, and put her first.

It was a pattern she desperately wanted to break. "It took a couple of years, but the fourth family that took me in when I was twelve was wonderful, and it was the first time I let my guard down and allowed myself to believe I was wanted. They had a daughter my age, and we were inseparable and best friends. After about a year in their care, they decided they wanted to adopt me."

"That's great," he said, though there was something about his too perceptive expression that told her he knew that things hadn't ended well.

"It *was* great," she agreed, remembering how elated she'd been when they'd told her the news, how safe and secure she'd felt for the first time since losing her entire family. "Until the husband got a job promotion that included moving to Germany. The Ackermans decided that it was too long and drawn out and complicated to go through the adoption process because of international laws, so they changed their minds. When they left for Germany, I was shuffled right back into the system."

He set his fork down on his empty plate and swore beneath his breath. She couldn't bring herself to glance across the table at him, to look into his eyes and see the pity she feared was reflected in his gaze.

After that heart-shattering rejection, she was never the same. Scared to trust anyone and afraid of becoming attached again, especially emotionally, she'd become withdrawn and had isolated herself, which in turn had made her a more difficult child to place. "I went through quite a few foster homes after that, and mostly the ones that were looking for a supplemental state paycheck instead of really wanting a child. When I turned eighteen and graduated from high school, I aged out of foster care and was completely on my own, with nowhere to go."

"What happened?" he asked softly.

She finally allowed herself to look at Levi, and the compassion and understanding she saw on his face gave her the courage to answer him. "I was homeless for a while, struggling to find a job, and it was hard and terrifying. A woman at the shelter where I was staying put me in contact with an organization called Foster Link that helps young adults just out of the system who are struggling to survive because they don't have a support system. They set me up with a caseworker, and she helped me get into an outreach housing program so I was no longer homeless. From there, we laid out a plan that included finding a job and focusing on a long-term career. Within a few weeks, I was working as a receptionist in a medical office, and I decided to take night classes at a local community college so I could work toward a nursing degree."

For the first time in her life, she'd felt as though

she'd finally found a path and had a direction, with a promising future. "Then about a year later, I met a guy at school. He was in my biology class, and after a few months of dating, I left the outreach housing program and we moved in together."

She couldn't even say that she'd loved James. She recognized now that her decision at the time had been more about her need for security and stability, and once again she'd believed she'd found that, this time with him. Except she'd discovered, belatedly, that James was all about himself, and he certainly hadn't stuck around when things had gotten rough.

"The office I was working at went out of business, which left me jobless again," she said as she absently slid her fingers along the condensation gathering on her glass while Levi listened silently. "And then one day, when I came home from an interview, all of James' things were gone, and so was he." He'd also taken all but ten dollars out of their joint savings account, leaving her flat broke, as well as unemployed. "So, I was on my own again. I had to drop out of school so I could work two jobs to get ahead, and, well, it's been a struggle ever since."

She couldn't bring herself to tell Levi about Dylan—that once again she'd allowed herself to think that he was different, that he cared about her . . . when the entire time he'd had ulterior motives, and once he'd lured her into Sacrosanct, he'd become a possessive asshole. That's when Sarah decided it was time to get out, any way she could.

"Sometimes, life *is* a struggle," Levi said, as if he'd gone through his share of strife. "But it doesn't always have to be that way."

She smiled at his comment, knowing he was trying to be positive. "I believe that, too. Which is part of the reason I'm leaving Chicago. I'm ready for a fresh start somewhere new, a clean slate, so to speak, and since I don't have anything or anyone tying me to this city, it's the perfect time to go."

"I get it," he said softly, though she could have sworn she saw a glimmer of regret in his gaze. "But as long as you're still here, there's always a chance that something might change your mind."

She shook her head. "I doubt it." Her mind was made up, and even a man as sexy and kind as Levi wouldn't detour her plans—not that he was offering her a reason to stay.

Things grew quiet, and she shifted in her chair and glanced down at her empty plate. "Dinner was wonderful. Thank you."

"I'm glad you liked it." He stood and picked up his dish. When she moved to do the same, he held out a hand to stop her before gathering her plate and utensils, too. "You stay right here. I'm just going to set these in the dishwasher and put away the leftovers. You ready for dessert? It's something decadent and chocolate."

She laughed and glanced up into his darkened green eyes, trying not to drown in their seductive depths. "You should know that I'm shameless when it comes to any kind of dessert. And if it's chocolate, then I'll be in heaven."

He grinned and winked at her. "One trip to heaven, coming up."

He went back into the kitchen, and she heard him at the sink as he cleaned up the dishes, then the sound of cupboard doors opening and closing, until he finally returned with two smaller plates.

She nearly moaned at the rich, indulgent dessert he set in front of her. "Did you make this?" she asked incredulously.

He laughed, the sound low and sexy as he sat across from her with his own slice of chocolate mousse cake. "No. My cooking skills don't extend to desserts. I bought it. But don't tell that to my sister-in-law, Samantha, who is a phenomenal pastry chef at one of those upscale bakeries downtown."

Sarah doubted she'd ever meet the woman. "My lips are sealed," she said, and took a bite of the melt-in-your-mouth cake, and this time, she did moan at the luscious texture and taste on her tongue.

Levi's heavy-lidded gaze zeroed in on her mouth from across the table, and even with the distance between them, it still felt like a physical caress. "That's the same sound you made when I kissed you," he pointed out huskily. "It's so fucking hot."

Her face flushed and she managed to swallow the bite in her mouth. "That's what happens when you feed me chocolate."

"I like it," he murmured, a bad-boy glint in his

eyes. "So if I kissed you while you were eating chocolate, do you think it would be an orgasmic experience for you?"

Yes, and her body agreed. Especially those neglected girly parts between her legs that pulsed and tingled at the thought of his mouth on hers again. Or on *any* part of her.

She tried to shake off the sensation, and because she really wanted to finish her dessert, she changed the subject for now. "You said your parents were gone," she said, touching on a topic he'd avoided earlier. "What happened?"

He arched a brow at her, seemingly disappointed that she hadn't taken him up on his orgasmic offer. "Tit for tat?"

She shrugged, and yeah, maybe she was taking advantage of the fact that she'd just spilled her past to him. "Fair is fair."

He didn't answer right away. Finally, he shook his head and scrubbed a hand along his jaw, that guarded look behind his eyes fading away. "Jesus, I don't even know where to start."

The raw, honest emotion written all over his face already made her heart constrict, because she suspected his story was just as painful as hers had been. "Let's start with your mother," she prompted gently. "How did she pass away?"

Again, he hesitated, just long enough for her to think he'd changed his mind about sharing, but then he spoke. "My mother was a prostitute and a junkie," he said, shocking her with his uncensored words. "For her, it was all about getting her next fix, so to pay for the drugs, she whored herself out. She didn't give a shit about any of her kids, and when I was around eight, she was arrested for drug possession and solicitation. It was her fifth offense on various charges, and she was sentenced to prison for eighteen months. She died of a stroke while she was incarcerated."

Sarah was so stunned she could only stare at him while she processed everything he'd just said. "Did your father raise you?" she asked since it was the most logical assumption.

His mouth twisted in a spiteful smile, even as he took a bite of his dessert. "The thing is, none of us boys knew who our fathers were since my mother got pregnant when she was with three different johns. We had a lot of abusive pricks who came through our lives because of my mother's addictions, but we *never* had a father figure."

So, he'd suffered as a child, just as she had, and it made her feel oddly connected to him. "Did the three of you end up in foster care?" She hated to ask but wanted to know what had happened to them.

He shook his head. "No. If it weren't for Clay, we would have definitely been split up. Somehow, someway, he was able to keep us together. He was sixteen at the time, and for the two years after that, he managed to keep all of us under the radar of social services while he worked odd jobs to support us. Like I said earlier, I ate a lot of macaroni and cheese and peanut butter and jelly sandwiches."

Sarah couldn't stop the emotional lump that formed in her throat. On one hand, she could totally relate to Levi's past and childhood, and on another, she knew that he and his brothers had gone through a whole different kind of hell. "I can't even imagine how difficult that was for all three of you."

"Clay obviously took the brunt of it all since he was the oldest. Mason, well, he was a goddamn hell-raiser who was a constant challenge for Clay. And me . . ." He shrugged, as if it didn't matter.

But what he'd endured *did* matter to her. And in a very short time, she'd already learned so much about Levi that she was able to finish his sentence for him. "You were the quiet, internal one, weren't you?"

Surprise flickered in his gaze that she'd pegged him so easily. "When you're constantly being threatened with 'be good or you'll be taken away,' it tends to scare the shit out of a kid. I was so afraid of never seeing my brothers again, and the only way I could deal with the chaos of everything going on around me was to keep my fears and emotions compartmentalized so they didn't completely overwhelm me."

She realized that even as a man, Levi still needed to maintain that control; he'd admitted as much earlier when she'd asked him about drinking alcohol and he'd said, *that lack of control is totally not my thing.* It all made sense and lined up with his in-charge personality. She was sure that being in the military had only intensified and solidified those traits.

"You mentioned you were in the service?" She figured he could use a break from the intensity of his story and hoped this part of his life had gone easier.

"Yeah. I was in the Army, as a military police officer." He casually leaned back in his chair, seemingly grateful to leave the childhood discussion behind. "Once I was discharged, it was a natural and easy transition to being a cop."

"Your choice of profession suits you," she said with a smile.

He tipped his head, his expression curious. "Yeah? How so?"

"I've known you for about five weeks now, almost six, and there is just an air of authority about you, without being overbearing," she said, thinking back on all the details she'd mentally collected on Levi during all his stops at Circle K and, more recently, when he'd been with his brothers. "You're honorable and loyal. And you're protective. You make me feel safe," she admitted softly. Due more to who he was as a man than him being a cop. And that revelation scared her, because she'd trusted other men in the past only to realize that sense of security had all been an illusion.

Levi's eyes darkened a shade as he studied her face, and even though he was sitting across the table, she shivered as though he'd intimately touched her. "Maybe I'm just protective of *you*."

The warm, sensual murmur of his voice added to the awareness suddenly thrumming through her. "You were just doing your job the other night at the store."

"Yes, I was," he agreed. "But that doesn't explain why I *still* feel protective of you. Why I want to physically remove you from that shitty job and make sure you're safe."

Oh, wow. The heat suddenly glimmering in his gaze made her shift in her chair, as did the tempting smile pulling at his mouth. Somehow, the atmosphere between them had changed, and her feminine senses were completely tuned in to his sex appeal.

She abruptly stood up and grabbed her empty dessert plate and fork. He started to join her, but this time she put her hand out to stop him, just as he'd done to her earlier. "You did the dinner dishes. The least I can do is the dessert plates." And good God, she needed a few minutes to subdue her disorderly hormones.

She escaped to the kitchen and washed the plates and forks, then set them on the dish rack. Just as she finished and intended to turn around, Levi came up behind her, so quietly that she jumped when he splayed his palms on either side of the sink so she couldn't escape, and oh-so-slowly pressed his body against the back of hers.

She closed her eyes and swallowed hard, unable to stop the rush of longing that worked its way through her system. She was deliciously trapped—in between his muscular arms and against the lean hips tucked against her ass—though she knew with even the slightest protest from her he'd back away. But he felt so damn good. So strong and warm and *real*. Resisting him was next to impossible, especially when he skimmed his lips across that bare, sensitive spot where her neck ended and her shoulder began.

Goose bumps rose all along her arms. "Levi, what are you doing?" she managed to utter, even as her head tipped to the left to give him more access to the side of her throat.

"I'm not done with dessert yet," he murmured against her ear. "And you, sweet Sarah, taste better than chocolate."

Chapter Five

S ARAH SHIVERED AT Levi's enticing words, especially when he followed up his husky comment by sliding his warm, damp tongue along her skin while pushing the strap of her dress and bra down her right arm, exposing more surface for him to taste. Another long, slow lick had her thighs clenching against the tingling sensation burgeoning between her legs, and when he gently sank his teeth into the tendons along her shoulder, she moaned as her entire body jolted from the deliciously arousing edge of pain he delivered.

Her nipples tightened into hard peaks that strained against the thin material of her dress, as if he'd plucked them directly with his fingers. She raised her hand to reach back so she could run her fingers through his hair, but he caught her wrist in a firm grasp before she could reach her destination. Guiding her arm back down, he flattened her palm on the edge of the counter.

"Do *not* move them again. The only hands that get to touch are *mine*," he said in a low, insistent growl near her ear. "Just relax and let me make you feel good."

Relaxing was impossible, but because she wanted to experience whatever pleasure Levi had to give, she didn't say a word, just let her body surrender to his seduction, which was incredibly easy for her to do—*with him*. She already knew he was a man who liked to be in charge, and she was quickly discovering that she was a woman who willingly—and shamelessly—responded to that dominant sexual edge she heard vibrating in his voice.

He slid his hand into her hair, and her heart rate accelerated as he slowly, gently twisted the strands around his fingers until he could control the movement of her head. He pulled it farther to the side and slightly back, completely exposing her entire neck, her throat, and the long line of her shoulder.

"Open your eyes, Sarah," he ordered softly. "There's something I want you to see."

As if he had her under his spell, she obeyed and lifted her heavy lashes, staring straight ahead since she was unable to look anywhere else. Her breath caught in her throat when she saw both of their reflections in the kitchen window. With the darkness outside, it was like looking in a mirror, enabling her to see his devastatingly masculine face beside hers—his intense features and incandescent eyes that gleamed with heat and lust.

"I want you to see how beautiful you are like this," he said, nipping at her lobe while his free hand glided along the curve of her waist. "All soft and willing and eager. You're so fucking perfect."

No, she wasn't perfect at all. Far from it. But right now, in this moment, she was going to believe that she was everything Levi wanted. Everything he needed. This was her fantasy to take with her once she was gone.

"You ready to come undone for me?" he asked, his voice dark with promise.

She had no idea what he intended to do to her, but there was no stopping the rush of excitement coursing through her, and she didn't hesitate with her answer. "Yes, please."

He chuckled, the wicked sound ramping up her anticipation even more. "You don't need to be so proper and polite with me, because there is *nothing* civilized about the things I want to do to you. Right now, it's all about your pleasure, so enjoy it, sweetheart."

His lips touched down on her neck again, slowly and gently at first, then with increasing pressure as he nuzzled his face along the side of her throat. She felt the light scrape of stubble on her flesh, a subtle burn that elicited another uninhibited moan from her. Unable to help herself, she closed her eyes to savor every thrilling sensation he evoked with his mouth— and good God, the man was incredibly adept at the kind of arousing neck kisses that made a woman a voluntary slave to his desires.

She was pliant and yielding to anything he wanted to do to her. Even when he released her hair and wrapped his hand around her throat and his fingers tightened slightly against her vocal chords—something that with any other guy would have flipped a warning switch—she allowed him to tip her head back even farther, until it was resting on his opposite shoulder. *That's* how much she trusted him.

Her back arched and her hips pushed provocatively against his. Through the thin material of her dress, she could feel the outline of his thick, rock-hard erection encased in denim as it pressed along the crease of her ass. With his body crowding hers against the counter, combined with the unrelenting way he held her, she was captured and restrained in the most thrilling, tantalizing way possible.

His lips moved along the curve of her neck, parted and damp, sucking and kissing, his own ragged breath on her flesh so hot she couldn't think straight. As if that weren't enough, he added the scraping and nibbling of his teeth, stimulating every single one of her erogenous zones and making her clit pulse with need.

Her breasts grew so full and tight they tingled, her nipples so hard they hurt. And when his sinful tongue joined in with long, sensual licks, she whimpered softly. Her thighs trembled, and damp heat pooled in intimate places, because now she knew just how thorough his mouth and tongue would feel between her legs. *Better than any man who had come before him.*

So many carnal sensations collided inside of her, and she started to pant, right on the verge of climaxing . . . *and how was that even possible from simple kisses to her neck?* Incredibly *erotic* kisses, but still, getting this revved up, this quickly, was not the norm for her. Then again, when had any guy taken the time and attention to indulge in this kind of lengthy foreplay? Never. And it was goddamn glorious.

"Levi," she gasped, shifting her bottom restlessly against what she wanted the most. Him. Inside her. Easing the ache he'd ignited. "You're making me so . . ." She couldn't bring herself to be that bold and say something so explicit.

"I'm making you so what?" he persisted huskily, his lips and voice vibrating against her neck while the fingers around her throat gently stroked the line of her jaw. "Weak in the knees?"

"That's one thing," she said, laughing lightly and opening her eyes again.

"Hot and bothered?" he suggested, then sucked and licked a path along her shoulder, making her moan like a hussy.

"Yes, that, too." She bit her bottom lip, not sure how much longer she was going to be able to stand this torment.

"How about *wet*, sweet thing?" He breathed hotly into her ear as he slipped his free hand beneath the hem of her dress and feathered his long, warm fingers along her inner thigh. "Is your pussy slick and hot and needy?" He stroked closer to the plain cotton panties that were undeniably soaked through, teasing her. "Do you need me to make you come?"

She swallowed hard and clutched the edge of the counter for support. Another thing she wasn't at all used to—dirty talk. But coming from Levi, it was hot and sexy and titillating *and she loved it.*

"*Answer me*, Sarah," he demanded in a low, curt tone as he flicked a finger along her bare inner thigh to get her attention.

She sucked in a startled breath as that light snap of pain seemed to reverberate against her clit. "Yes," she said quickly. "Oh, God, yes."

"Yes, *what?*" he asked impatiently as his fingers flexed around her throat and his mouth skimmed her cheek. "I'm not touching your soft, quivering pussy until you ask for it."

He moved his hand to the waistband of her underwear and stopped there, the heat of his palm against her lower belly a brand against her skin. Sarah's sex felt heavy, swollen, and the thought of him leaving her like this, in a state of churned-up lust, made her more brazen than she'd ever been before. She rolled her head against his shoulder so that she was looking up at him, staring into eyes that were so dark and hungry—for her.

"Put your fingers on my clit, Levi," she rasped desperately, knowing he'd accept no less than the filthy version. "Touch me, stroke me, make me come, *please.*"

"Good girl," he murmured as if she'd passed some kind of unspoken test.

Finally giving her body what it craved, he slid his hand into her panties and right down between her legs, drawing a startled gasp from her. As soon as he encountered her slick, wet heat, his fingers stilled in her plump folds as he groaned, his body shuddering hard against hers. "Jesus Christ, Sarah." The words sounded torn from his throat. "You're absolutely soaked and so fucking soft."

"Don't stop, Levi," she pleaded as she frantically rolled her hips against his hand, urging it to *move*. "*Please*, don't stop."

He swore again and pushed his fingers deep between her aching flesh and dragged them back through her slit, until he was pressing and rubbing against her clit and pushing her toward the cataclysmic release building frantically inside of her. With his other hand still at her throat, she tipped her head back to once again meet his tempestuous gaze. His jaw was clenched, his entire body tense, and the untamed need blazing in his eyes was contagious, making her catch fire, too.

She writhed against the hand pleasuring her and moaned desperately, the breathy sounds slipping past her lips over and over again. "Levi . . ."

"*Fuck*. That is where I want my mouth," he rasped, his eyes lit from within as his fingers relentlessly worked her over. "I want to lick you and eat you and taste you on my tongue as you come. Then I want to slid my cock into your soft, tight pussy and bury myself so fucking deep that you scream my name."

Those were the last words she heard as he pulled her mouth up to his and kissed her, hard and deep, giving her no choice but to reciprocate as his lips conquered and devoured. His tongue swirled over and around hers, mimicking the way his fingers circled her clit, pushing her into the sweetest, most exquisite oblivion.

She bucked against him, her body quaking as she climaxed so hard she screamed against his lips, the contractions taking her higher and over an edge she'd never imagined existed. And when she was finally able to think, she wondered if she'd ever be the same again.

Finally, he released her mouth and dropped his hand from her throat. She sagged like a rag doll against the counter, her head falling forward as she tried to gain her bearings. He was still standing behind her, his hands now on her hips, gently but firmly enough to hold her upright so she didn't sink to the floor.

"You okay?" he asked, humor lacing his deep, husky voice.

"Umm, I think so," she replied, her heart rate finally slowing and her breathing returning to normal. "That was so . . . intense."

"And you were fucking amazing," he said, trailing his hands along her waist.

Except while she'd just enjoyed a phenomenal orgasm, he was still hard as granite against her bottom, and just feeling the imprint of that impressive cock made her want *more* of him than just his fingers pleasuring her.

She turned in his arms, and while he gave her enough room to move, he didn't step away. He still stood close, the corner of his mouth tipped with a smug, self-satisfied smile.

She knew what she wanted to ask him, but she'd never propositioned a man before, and she suddenly felt awkward, considering what he'd just done to her. "Do you want to . . . umm, go in the bedroom and . . ."

He took pity on her graceless attempt to seduce him and shook his head. "Not tonight." He tenderly tucked a few strands of her hair behind her ear, a touch of regret glimmering in his gaze. "But make no mistake, there isn't anything I want more than to strip you naked and spread you out on my bed, then drive so deep inside of your body that there's nothing else you can do but take every single inch of me."

His words inflamed her all over again and confused her. "If that's what we *both* want, then why not?" Because the truth was, there most likely wasn't going to be another night with Levi. She'd agreed to one date for a reason—it kept things between them simple and uncomplicated when it was time for her to go. Except the way her heart tightened at the thought of leaving this man behind, she feared she was already falling for him.

"Ahhh, Sarah," he said on a soft sigh as he traced a

finger along her jaw. "You have such a sweet innocence about you, and I'm not sure you're ready for me."

She blinked up at him. How could he say that after the way she'd just responded to him? Her body was primed and ready and oh-so-willing, and it wasn't as though she was a virgin, for crying out loud, and she made that clear. "I'm not innocent when it comes to sex."

He arched a dark blonde brow at her that was filled with a quiet challenge. "You are when it comes to *my* kind of sex."

"Which is?"

"Let's just say . . . that issue I have about being in control? It extends to what happens in the bedroom and what I want to do to you while we're in there."

She licked her bottom lip as her imagination went into overdrive, the erotic visions filling her mind so hot and exciting that she had to suppress a shiver. "I'm okay with that."

"Are you absolutely sure? Because I'm not a gentle lover." His lips twisted with an almost perverse smile as he gripped her hips again and pulled her forward so that the ridge of his erection reminded her how much he had to give—clearly more than the average man.

"Are you okay with being restrained to my bed while I have access to every part of your naked body to do whatever I want? And just to be clear, I want you on your hands and knees so I can grab and smack your ass while I pound into you, so goddamn hard and deep it'll shove you up the mattress a few feet and you'll forget your own name. I want you on your back, your legs spread indecently wide, with my mouth and tongue and fingers fucking you before I take you with my cock. And when you think you can't take any more, I'm going to want to do it all over again."

Oh. My. God. With every descriptive detail he shared, she felt her eyes growing wide—in shock and, Lord help her, with anticipation of experiencing that darker part of Levi that made him the complex man he was. She understood that now.

He lifted his hand and dragged the pad of his thumb along her lower lip before pressing it inside until she tasted his warm, salty skin. "And this sweet, soft, innocent mouth of yours? I want to do dirty, filthy things to it. I want to see it swallow every bit of my cock as I push my way to the back of your throat. I want to feel it suck me dry as I come."

A soft whimpering sound bubbled its way out of her, and she had to resist the urge to drop to her knees and *let him* do those hot, indecent things. *When had she become so shameless?* Even as the thought crossed through her mind, she knew that Levi was the reason. No other man had ever made her feel so uninhibited.

His perceptive gaze swept across her features, and a sexy, knowing smile curved his mouth. "You're breathing hard, your face is flushed, and your nipples are nice and tight against your dress, so your body clearly likes the idea of giving me everything I want and need." He drew a shuddering breath, letting her know he wanted those things, too. "But not tonight," he said, disappointing her when he remained firm on that decision. "We're not going there until I know for sure that you're ready mentally and being with me won't freak you out."

"Have you freaked out other women?" she asked, not because she was afraid, but she was definitely curious.

His chuckle was low and spontaneous. "No, but then I've always chosen my sexual partners very carefully. You, Sarah Robins, are the exception."

With that revelation hanging in the air, he stepped away from her and pushed the tips of his hands into the front pockets of his jeans. "I've given you more than enough to think about tonight, so how about I take you home and we revisit this discussion on our second date?"

She opened her mouth to respond to that, but he quickly cut her off before she could speak.

"Before you remind me that you aren't going to be around for long, for the time that you *are* here in Chicago, can you keep an open mind about . . . *us*?" He met her gaze, his intention serious and persuasive.

He was so damn tempting, and he certainly wasn't asking for forever. Hell, he'd just given her a very explicit rundown of exactly what his interest in her was. He was offering a temporary affair—albeit a scorching-hot one with him implicitly in control—and before she could change her mind, she replied with an encouraging but not fully committed, "Maybe."

He laughed, humor deepening his tone. "Not quite a yes and not quite a no. But it's definitely an answer I can work with."

Chapter Six

STILL STANDING IN the kitchen, Levi scrubbed a hand along his jaw, watching Sarah as she walked down the hallway that led to the bathroom. Her absence gave him a couple of minutes to process everything that had happened in the past few hours. Not just the kissing and orgasm that had nearly sent him over the edge with the need to feel those rippling contractions around his cock, but their deep, intimate conversations at dinner, the sharing that had given him greater insight into her painfully rough life, and mostly, how his feelings for Sarah Robins were escalating at a shockingly rapid rate.

The thought should have panicked him. He didn't let women past those barriers protecting his heart, but he'd already run the gamut of emotions with her. He'd gone from flirtatious interest to concerned and caring to wanting to protect her from anything and everything in life that could harm her. With any other woman, he'd be quick to cut ties at the tiniest shift in his feelings, but there was something delicate and vulnerable about Sarah that made him want to pull her closer, not push her away.

Maybe it was the similarities in their pasts, the way they'd both grown up without parents to nurture and guide them. At least he'd had Clay as a role model and someone who'd busted his ass to make sure the three of them weren't separated by social services, but Sarah . . . To think that she'd lost loving parents to a house fire, then had been abandoned by another family she believed wanted her, broke his heart . . . and made him want to be the one to mend it all at the same time.

He'd known her for nearly six weeks, and what had started as friendly and flirtatious stop-ins at the Circle K had evolved into him wanting *more*. Sexually, yeah, he wanted to corrupt that innocence and make her his own private dirty girl, which he knew without a doubt she had hidden inside her. She hadn't flinched or stared at him in horror when he'd laid all his predilections on the table, and she accepted his need for control. In fact, he'd seen the distinct fascination in her gaze, and *fuck*, tamping down the urge not to drag her off to his bedroom and follow through with every salacious thing he'd suggested to her had been damned near impossible.

But this went beyond simple attraction. She was the first woman to stir something deep inside of him when he honestly thought that part of him was damaged beyond repair. He was undeniably drawn to that sweet innocence he'd spoken of, that sensitive nature of hers that told him she was less jaded about people and their motives than him—despite what she'd been through. While he tended to choose women he deemed safe and easy to walk away from, the mere thought of Sarah walking away from *him* made his stomach twist with something way too possessive.

When she'd casually mentioned her plan to leave town when he'd picked her up earlier, he'd had to deliberately steel his expression so she couldn't see the panic flashing through him at the notion of losing her before he'd ever had her. Then he'd gone and pushed her for a second date when he knew she was trying to keep things between them from becoming too en-twined.

He exhaled a harsh breath and leaned his hip against the counter, silently berating himself for being a selfish asshole—because if he really had a shred of decency in him, he'd cut Sarah loose instead of pursu-ing her any further, and not just because she wanted to leave. He'd never been able to give *any* woman more than sex, so what made him think he had the ability to give Sarah what she needed emotionally?

Even for the short time she remained here, she deserved better than a fucked-up man who carried around too much bitterness from his past. He'd been forced to keep horrible secrets from his brothers that no five-year-old boy should have seen or endured. He'd buried all those repulsive, disturbing memories as deep as he could, but they were always there in the back of his mind, haunting him like a ghost. No matter how hard he tried to forget, the anger and resentment would never be completely gone, and he knew without a doubt his mother's actions, on more than one occasion, had destroyed his ability to believe in love.

But even knowing he carried around a shit-ton of baggage, Levi *still* couldn't bring himself to let Sarah go. And he wasn't prepared to think about her leaving him until the time came and he was forced to do so.

"I'm ready," Sarah said as she came back into the kitchen. She took one look at his face, and worry creased her brows. "Is everything okay?"

God, she was already so tuned in to his moods, when he was normally very adept at keeping his emotions under wraps. "I'm good," he lied, wanting to leave the past where it belonged. He picked up his truck keys and gave her a smile. "Let's get you home."

A few minutes later, they were in his vehicle and had just turned out of his neighborhood when he cast a quick glance across the cab at her. "Which direction to your place?"

She fidgeted in her seat and wouldn't look at him. "Umm, you can just drop me off at the store."

He wasn't surprised that Sarah was insisting he leave her at the Circle K where he'd picked her up a couple of hours ago, but the night that he'd gotten shot, as a cop he'd noticed something before heading into the store. There had been no other cars parked anywhere near or around the mart, and with only

Sarah working, he remembered wondering where *her* vehicle was. And then everything had escalated so quickly with the robbery, and that thought had been the last thing on his mind.

But now, he wasn't about to take her in that direction until she assured him of a few things first. "Do you have a car there?"

She hesitated, and even though he suspected her answer, he pushed for it. "Sarah, answer me."

She glanced out the passenger window. "No, I don't have a car, but a friend is going to pick me up."

The words came out of her in a rush—the same exact excuse she'd given Clay that night at the hospital when he'd offered her a ride home. Had she made even the slightest effort to look him in the eyes, Levi *might* have believed her about the friend. But he'd been a cop long enough to recognize the signs that she wasn't being truthful—her delayed responses, the fact that she'd yet to meet his gaze, the unsteady tone of her voice—all instinctively told him that she was hiding something. It wasn't the first time he'd gotten that impression, and he was betting that whatever secrets she was keeping all tied into her less-than-desirable job that undoubtedly only paid minimum wage, her insistence that she was leaving the city soon, and now, her issue with him driving her *directly* home.

"I'll give my friend a call as soon as I'm at the mart, so you don't have to wait around," she told him as she clasped and unclasped her hands in her lap in a nervous gesture.

"*Don't,*" he said, and while his voice was soft, there was no mistaking the warning in his tone.

Finally, she glanced at him, her body language and the wide-eyed look in her gaze filled with distinct wariness. "Don't what?"

Fuck. He gripped the steering wheel hard. With his patience hanging by a thin thread, he found a legal parking spot on the street and pulled over to the curb. He put the truck into park and turned his entire body toward her, trying to keep his frustration at a manageable level.

"Don't lie to me, Sarah. *Ever,*" he said gruffly, wanting her to trust him with whatever was going on in her life. "Starting right now with the answer to my question. How do you get to work every day and home every night?"

Those full lips he'd ravished not so long ago pursed ever so slightly, and she looked him directly in his eyes. "I take the bus." She shrugged a shoulder. "It's not a big deal."

It was a *big* fucking deal to *him* when she was being dropped off at a bus stop in a shitty part of town and still had to walk to the store or wherever the hell she lived.

"*I'm* taking you home, because I'm not letting you get on a goddamn bus this late at night." It drove him crazy to think she took public transportation all alone after midnight and *anything* could happen to her. "Give me your address."

She shook her head, her expression obstinate.

"No. I've been on my own a long time and I can take care of myself."

He knew that was true based on what she'd shared with him earlier, but he couldn't deny the protective instincts she stirred in him. Being in law enforcement, it was his duty to defend people, but he'd *never* been one to get involved in a woman's life who he was dating, or dictate the things she did. Again, Sarah was quickly becoming the exception to every goddamn rule he'd set for himself.

"This isn't a choice, Sarah," he said, knowing he was far more stubborn and tenacious than she could ever be, and he wasn't backing down. "I want to make sure that you get home *safely*, so this isn't going to happen any other way. Where do you live?"

She glared at him and crossed her arms over her chest defensively. "You want to know where I live?" She asked the question like a dare. "Fine. Let me show you."

She gave him an address in Englewood that he calmly punched into his navigation system, even as he was silently thinking in his head, *Jesus fucking Christ.* Levi knew the general area was a wasteland for all levels of crime, and it was no place for a single, vulnerable woman to live.

As he started driving again, Sarah opted to remain quiet and kept her gaze averted. Yeah, she was pissed at him for being so pushy, but when it came to her well-being, he didn't give a rat's ass. Her welfare was his main concern and priority.

He followed the directions on his GPS as the little arrow took them through a low-income, gang-infested area and brought them closer and closer to their destination. A block away from the address, Levi stopped at a red light and glanced through the wind-shield to see what was up ahead on the right-hand side. A sickening sensation swirled in the pit of his stomach when he caught sight of the two-story Sleepy Time Motel and the brightly lit VACANCY sign. Illumi-nated below that was the draw for any prostitute, drug addict, and other unsavory activities: *Hourly rates available.*

No fucking way. He'd busted a few drug dealers and hookers at this run-down location, and Jesus Christ, he wanted to believe there was some kind of mistake with the address, but when the light turned green and he started driving forward, it was Sarah who confirmed his worst fears.

"You can drop me off at the curb in front of the motel," she said quietly. "I can walk to my room from there."

He gave her a quick, incredulous glance, trying like hell to remain calm and level-headed when his entire body vibrated with anger—not at Sarah but the situation.

"That's not a fucking option," he said, his tone un-compromising as he turned the truck into the driveway of the motel. He wasn't letting her out of his sight until she was locked in her room, and even then he didn't know if he could truly drive away and leave her alone. "Where is your room?"

"Around back. Lower level. Room 116," she said in a reluctant voice so low he could barely hear her.

As he drove through the parking lot, he had to physically swallow back the bile rising in his throat as he thought about someone as defenseless as Sarah *living* in this dangerous environment *every single day*. On top of that, this fucking dump of a place was an inescapable reminder of all the times his mother had forced him to witness her own disgusting and despicable lifestyle—turning tricks for cash, which she would then turn around and hand over to the closest drug dealer for a fix instead of feeding the hungry five-year-old boy she'd brought with her. He'd be close by while she did revolting things to strangers, and she'd threatened him to be quiet, to never tell his brothers or else he'd be taken away.

Yeah, great fucking memories there.

He made his way around to the back of the dimly lit motel and pulled his vehicle into a parking spot. He cut the engine and turned toward Sarah, grabbing her wrist just as she tried to unbuckle her seat belt. She glanced at him sharply, and there was just enough illumination in the cab for him to see her flushed face and how angry she was . . . on the outside. But beneath that fuming emotion, he saw the real truth in her eyes that reflected shame and humiliation.

He swore beneath his breath. "What the hell, Sarah? Why are you living here?"

"It's all I can afford," she said, her chin lifting willfully. "I'm just trying to get through a few more weeks until I have enough money to leave. And it's better than living on the streets."

As much as he admired her strength and fortitude, it killed him inside to know this is what she came home to every night. And for some reason, she obviously didn't have anyone else she could turn to. Certainly no family to speak of. "Let me help you, Sarah. If you need money or—"

"No." She cut him off and pulled her hand from his grasp. "I don't need any handouts or you feeling sorry for me. I've been in worse situations than this, and I've been absolutely fine staying here."

She unbuckled her seat belt, and short of cuffing her—which he seriously considered—he knew there was no stopping Sarah from getting out of the vehicle. He quickly reached into the glove box and retrieved his service revolver, which he'd placed in there earlier before picking her up at the store. He never went far without his weapon and normally had it holstered at his side beneath his shirt, but he hadn't wanted to freak her out if she touched it while he was kissing her—because yeah, he'd known that first kiss in his kitchen was going to happen.

Her eyes widened as she caught sight of the gun, and when her gaze lifted to his, he pinned her with a firm look. "Keep your ass right where it is until I come around and get you," he said, not missing the annoyance that flashed in her eyes.

Satisfied that she wasn't going to argue or defy him, even if she didn't care for his order, he got out of his side of the truck, his gaze automatically scanning his surroundings as he tucked his weapon into the back waistband of his jeans. There was no one in this back area at the moment, but the parking lot and around his vehicle was littered with condom wrappers, used syringes, and drug paraphernalia.

Fucking great.

By the time Levi reached the passenger side and helped her out, he was silently seething—again, because of Sarah's predicament and her stubborn refusal to accept any help. Keeping a hand on the base of her spine and her stiff, tension-filled body tucked close, he let her lead the way to her room. He stood behind her as she retrieved a keycard and swiped it, then opened the door and stepped inside.

Before he had a chance to follow, a soft, horrified cry escaped her, and she suddenly moved in reverse until her backside collided against the front of his body. He caught her by the upper arms to steady her, but he felt her trembling. One glance over her shoulder into the room, which was illuminated by the dim lamp on the nightstand, and he realized why. The place had been completely ransacked—the mattress had been pulled from the box spring, pillows had been ripped open, and the dresser drawers were open haphazardly and had been rifled through.

Reacting quickly and instinctively, Levi pushed Sarah back against the wall by the door and withdrew his gun. The room was small, without many places for a perp to hide, and it took him less than a minute to check the tiny closet, then do a sweep of the compact bathroom. Someone had removed the lid from the toilet, and he noticed that the window had been busted open. The frame was big enough for someone to climb through, and Levi suspected that it had most likely been a random burglary. That someone had known she was out for the evening and broken in with hopes of finding cash or something of value.

But as he walked back into the bedroom, it was clear that Sarah didn't have much, let alone something of financial worth. She'd told him that things had been rough for a while, but this . . . this was near destitute. There were only a few clothes hanging in the closet, and the drawers contained bare necessities. Even the food tossed onto the floor was basic and cheap—and reminded him of the kind of groceries Clay had bought for him and Mason to fill their hungry bellies: ramen, oatmeal, off-brand granola bars, and peanut butter. *Fuck.*

He made his way back to Sarah, and since there was no imminent threat, he returned his weapon to the waistband of his jeans. Her face was pale, she was visibly shaking, and she looked at him with legitimate fear in her tear-filled eyes.

"They . . . they took the . . . TV and microwave," she stuttered out, clearly in shock.

Levi didn't give a shit about any of that, and tomorrow he'd deal with reporting the break-in and robbery to the manager of the motel. Right now, his only concern was getting Sarah out of this fucking hellhole once and for all.

Chapter Seven

LEVI COULDN'T SLEEP. Not a big surprise considering everything that had happened this evening. He tucked his hands behind his head and stared up at the shadows flitting across the ceiling, his mind jam-packed with so many thoughts it was difficult to process them all. But there was at least one thing he didn't have to worry about any longer, and that was knowing Sarah was safe—in his house and sleeping in one of the spare bedrooms down the hall. *Thank God.*

He'd been so damned relieved she hadn't argued with him when he'd ordered her to pack up her belongings, *all of them*, because she wouldn't be returning. Then again, she'd been in a traumatized state, moving around the room as if she were operating on autopilot. All of her clothes and personal items had fit into a regular-sized backpack, a thought that pained him. And when she'd gone into the bathroom and seen the lid off the toilet, she'd spiraled into total panic—and he'd had no clue why.

Her breathing had escalated, her body shook, and huge tears welled in her eyes as she murmured, "*No, no, no,*" over and over again, until he finally grabbed her arms and demanded to know what was wrong.

With a huge, defeated sob, she'd told him she'd had a little over three hundred dollars she'd kept in a Ziploc bag in the tank for safe-keeping. It was all the cash she had to her name, gone now, most likely in the hands of some junkie who was wise to that particular trick. He'd taken her into his arms and promised everything would be okay, and even now, he swore it would be . . . if she'd just let him help her.

But now that the crisis was over, Levi couldn't help but analyze Sarah's situation. He tried to take all he knew about her dire circumstances and put them all together like pieces of a puzzle to form a complete story. All those scenarios didn't make for a pretty picture: the minimal way she'd lived, the job she worked, the type of food she'd bought, her meager belongings, and even how she'd hidden all her cash because she didn't have a bank account—they were a perfect setup for someone to pick up and disappear at a moment's notice. If he was a gambling man, he'd bet everything he owned that she was running from someone or something.

He'd considered pressing her for answers once he'd gotten her home, but her anxiety level was so high, her mood so agitated, he'd made her take a warm shower, then drink a glass of wine, before putting her in the guest bed down the hall from his.

And when she'd looked up at him with blue eyes that were so sad and lost and whispered, "I'm so sorry," for something that wasn't even her fault, he'd felt his heart twist hard and sharp in his chest. He'd slid into bed beside her, taken her into his arms, and held her tight. Returning to his own room hadn't been easy.

Now that he was calmer and more rational, he realized that forcing her to explain her situation, *all of it*, would be the quickest way to push her away. If he'd learned anything about Sarah, it was that she had a lot of pride and didn't like to rely on anyone for anything. Once she woke up and realized she was at his mercy with nowhere to go, she'd be defensive and wary. He needed to back off, not push harder.

It went against every one of his instincts as both a man and a cop to back down, but that same intuition told him to tread slowly and carefully or she'd run from him, too. The best he could do was to keep her safe and protected, without any demands, and hopefully she'd come around and trust him with the real truth.

The sound of soft footsteps padding down the hall pulled him from his thoughts. He glanced toward his open bedroom door just as Sarah's slender figure appeared in the frame.

Concerned, he moved off the bed and went to her. "Hey," he said softly, taking her hand in his. "Is everything okay?"

Moonlight streamed through the uncovered window, lighting the delicate angles of her face, and the anguish in her eyes sliced right through him, sharp as a knife.

"Yes . . . no." Her voice was small, her expression uncertain as she shifted anxiously on her bare feet before saying more. "I don't want to be by myself tonight. Can I sleep in here with you?"

Refusing her didn't even cross his mind. In fact, *he'd* sleep better knowing she was right beside him, where he could keep an eye on her and see for himself at any given moment that she was resting peacefully.

"Of course you can stay with me," he said, and with her hand still clasped in his, he led her to the other side of the bed.

He pulled back the covers, watching as she crawled onto the mattress wearing a threadbare tank top and equally old and worn sleep shorts. Clearly, her pajamas had seen better days, and the thin material did little to conceal her small, firm breasts and the too slender curve of her hips and ass.

Having her in his bed tonight wasn't about sex, but that didn't stop his dick from sitting up and taking notice of her tight nipples and those smooth legs he'd love to feel wrapped around his waist as he plowed deep inside of her.

He swallowed back a groan before it could slip from his throat and beat back the provocative thoughts that would only lead to a hard-on and a restless night's sleep. Once she was settled beneath the comforter, he walked around to his side of the bed and rolled to his side. Their heads were on separate pillows, but they were facing one another, less than a foot of space between them.

"I really am sorry, Levi," she said quietly, though he could still hear the wealth of regret in her voice. "I keep causing you a lot of trouble."

"How so?"

She tucked her hands beneath her cheek, her brows pinched in a frown. "The robbery at the store and you getting shot, for one thing," she reminded him.

"Awww, that was nothing more than a little bruise," he said, grinning playfully in an attempt to lighten the conversation.

She didn't smile as he'd hoped. "And you having to bring me back to your place so I have somewhere to stay for the night."

"Not just for the night, Sarah," he said as he reached out and caressed his thumb tenderly along her jaw. "For as long as you need."

"It won't be long," she insisted in a raspy voice that was steeped in emotion. "I swear it won't be."

"I don't care if it is," he said, realizing how true that was—how quickly he'd come to care about her. And how much he wanted her, and more than just physically. "There's no time limit on my offer."

"Thank you," she whispered, as if he'd just given her a precious gift.

He watched tears of gratitude shimmer in her eyes, and she swallowed hard. He suspected she wasn't used to someone giving anything without demanding something in return. Or just kindness in general. As a kid of a known drug addict and crack whore, he hadn't had a whole lot of kindness in his young life, either, but as an adult, at least he was surrounded by good, decent people he could count on if he needed anything at all.

Sarah didn't seem to have that luxury.

He wanted to be that person for her, the one who protected her and chased away her demons, real or imagined. He wanted to be the man she could turn to. And right now, he understood what he could offer— *comfort and a sense of security in the midst of her unstable life.*

He gently grabbed her arm and pulled her toward him. "Come here and let me hold you."

With a soft, inarticulate sound, she moved quickly and scrambled across the short distance between them. Clinging to him like a lifeline, she buried her face against his naked chest. He wrapped an arm around her shoulders and pulled her closer, the warmth of his body absorbing the chill from hers.

"God, I'm such a mess," she said, and he felt her wet tears on his skin. "My life is such a mess."

He ran his free hand through her hair and placed a tender kiss on her forehead. "You're not a mess, Sarah."

She laughed harshly against his neck, as if he had no idea what her life was like, and it irked him that he didn't. Not really.

"All that money gone . . . and now I have to start

saving all over again."

She sounded so defeated, but her comment gave him an opening to gently prod for deeper answers, and he went with it. "Saving for what, sweetheart?"

"To leave." Her arms tightened around his waist, as if to contradict the words she'd just spoken by holding on to him. "I need to leave."

"Why do you need to leave?" he asked calmly, when he really wanted to demand, *what are you running from?*

She shook her head. "Because I do."

Levi didn't get any of the answers he sought, but eventually she relaxed against him, falling asleep in his arms. He stayed up much longer, hoping like hell that he'd be able to figure out a way to change her mind about leaving Chicago.

About leaving *him.*

SARAH GRADUALLY WOKE up early the following morning, momentarily confused as to why she was cuddled up to a warm male body in a bed that was soft and comfortable—unlike the stiff, hard, and foul-smelling mattress she'd been sleeping on for the past month and a half. She gradually opened her eyes, and it took her a few moments to wrap her mind around her surroundings, and when she did, the horrible memories of last night came flooding back in an overwhelming wave of despair.

Yet here she was, safe and protected in Levi's

home, snuggled against him with her head resting on his chest. Her ear was pressed against his heart, and the sound of each steady beat calmed and lulled her. It was the first time in forever that she truly felt secure and relaxed, instead of waking up and being cautious and guarded about *everything* from the moment her eyes popped open.

But as grateful as she was for Levi's comfort last night, and his offer to stay with him for as long as she needed, she didn't want to be a burden or a responsibility to him. Clearly, he was a man who was used to living alone and on his own. She just needed a few days, a week at the most, to get some money together again and figure out a plan. Then she'd be on her way. Every day that she stayed in Chicago was another day for Dylan to find her.

Her stomach clenched at the knowledge, because she knew with certainty that he'd take her right back to Sacrosanct regardless of her protests, even if it meant he did so against her will. And once she was locked behind those steel gates again, there was no doubt in her mind that there wouldn't be another chance to escape the cult-like community. Not when she was already facing punishment for being a deserter.

But right now, in this quiet, peaceful moment, she didn't want to think about anything except Levi and how much she wanted him. Especially after the way he'd seduced her in the kitchen with his arousing kisses and a toe-curling orgasm, she mused with a smile that chased away those darker thoughts of

Dylan. She wanted to return the favor and make Levi feel good, too. And if it led to more . . . she wouldn't complain. He'd already warned her about his erotic preferences, and there wasn't anything about Levi that scared her—certainly not his need to be in control or his penchant for hot, dirty, rough sex.

She had a leg draped over one of his thighs and an arm secured around his waist. Closing her eyes, she placed her hand on his bare chest and slowly skimmed her palm down his torso, careful to stay away from the bruise on his lower left-hand side.

His breathing pattern immediately changed, growing deeper, heavier, as if he was waking up and realizing that *he* was being seduced this time around. She used her fingers to trace the indentations along his muscular abs and glided them even lower, until she reached the waistband of the cotton gym shorts he'd worn to bed.

Beneath her ear, his heart rate increased, and her own pulse thrummed through her veins as she slid her fingers beneath that elastic band. Her fingertips immediately brushed across the thick, taut head of a substantial erection, but before she could stroke his length, Levi released a feral growl and grasped her wrist. He pulled her hand from his shorts, and in the next moment, he had her flat on her back with his body half on top of hers so she was pinned beneath him.

He anchored her one arm above her head as he stared down at her, his green eyes bright, hot, and very, very lucid. "You're heading into dangerous territory," he warned huskily.

"I know," she whispered. She wanted to forget everything else in her life at the moment so she could give herself over to passion and just *feel*.

His jaw clenched, and she knew he was contemplating the situation, possibly over thinking it, and she didn't want to give him the chance to refuse her again.

"I want you, Levi." She licked her bottom lip anxiously. "Please."

He swore beneath his breath, but to her relief, he didn't reject her as she feared. Instead, he abruptly moved and straddled her thighs, trapping her beneath his weight. She looked up at him, so devastatingly gorgeous and sexy with a body made for sin. He exuded pure male confidence and had the physical power to back it up. He made her weak with wanting and damp with desire.

He braced his hands on either side of her head, his gaze direct and intense as it met hers. "If we're doing this, we're doing it *my* way. Do you understand?"

His way was all about being in charge and her surrendering to his control. He'd made that irrefutably clear last night, so there was no misunderstanding his intent now. Anticipation made her breathless, and excitement caused her nipples to tighten into aching points beneath the scratchy material of her tank top. The lust that flared in his gaze told her that he'd noticed both.

"Yes, I understand," she said, nodding eagerly.

A slow, sinful smile curved his mouth as he pushed up the hem of her tank top, then pulled it up and over her head and off. He sat up, tossing the piece of clothing to the floor while his gaze seemingly devoured her small but firm breasts. While he was momentarily distracted, it gave her a quick opportunity to glance down his body, to the long, thick column of flesh pushing insistently against his cotton shorts. The thought of so much cock stretching her and filling her beyond anything she'd experienced so far made her shiver. And when she finally dragged her gaze back up to his, there was no mistaking the knowing and slightly arrogant smirk on his lips.

"Put both of your hands above your head and keep them there," he ordered, and waited for her to comply.

She lifted her arms and placed them on the pillow above her head, palms up and open. The prone position stretched her upper body, making her feel surprisingly sensual and brazen in a way she'd never been before. Still sitting astride her hips, he splayed his hands on her flat stomach and slowly glided them up her torso, causing a soft sigh of pleasure to escape her lips. When he reached her breasts, he squeezed them together and swept his thumbs over her tight, sensitive nipples before lightly pinching and rolling them between his fingers.

She gasped and arched her back, shocked by how the slight jolt of pain had the ability to deliver a flood of heat and moisture between her legs. Shocked, too, by how much it turned her on when he plucked at the hard, nerve-laced peaks once again.

With her breasts still filling his hands, he pushed them up as he lowered his head and flicked his tongue across a stiff nipple before pulling it hard and deep into his mouth. She made a soft mewling sound as he sucked on her, as his tongue swirled and his teeth scraped across the now tender flesh until she was aroused beyond belief. She pressed her hips upward, undulating against the muscled thighs still straddling her lower body, desperate to ease the building, throbbing need expanding inside her.

In his own sweet time, his mouth gradually moved down her quivering stomach, leaving a hot, damp trail of kisses in his wake. When he reached the waistband of her sleep shorts and panties, he quickly stripped them all the way off, then knelt between her legs. His hands smoothed their way up the insides of her thighs, pushing them wide open and baring all of her to his heated, lust-filled gaze.

"Do you remember what I told you last night?" he murmured, watching as he pushed his thumbs through the plump folds of her weeping sex—from her clit all the way down to her core, then back up again.

She was slick from arousal, swollen, aching, and with each swipe of his fingers along her slit, she was quickly losing the ability to concentrate on anything other than the way he touched her. "Which part?" she panted, unable to recall anything specific when he had her so restless and needy.

He bent his head and gently bit the inside of her

thigh, making her gasp and arch her back again. "The part where I said that I want to lick this sweet pussy and eat you and taste you on my tongue as you come."

His words alone made her shudder. She could only imagine how her body would respond when he followed through on his promise. "Oh, God, yes. I remember."

"That's exactly what's going to happen, sweetheart," he said as he settled himself more comfortably between her spread limbs.

He arranged one leg, then the other, over his broad shoulders, then blew a hot stream of air across her wet folds. She bit her bottom lip and moaned, her entire body trembling in anticipation.

He slid his big, warm hands up to her hips, gripping them tightly with his fingers, securing her with his hold. "If just my breath on your pussy makes you quiver, can you imagine what my tongue will do?"

She didn't want to imagine, she wanted to *feel it.* "Show me," she whispered wantonly.

He immediately placed his hot, open mouth on her sex, devouring her until she squirmed and moaned—and belatedly realized that she wasn't prepared for the impact of this man's oral skills. Or her wild, shameless response to something so decadent. It took every ounce of restraint for her to keep her hands above her head and not reach down to grip his hair with her fingers. As much as she wanted to lower her arms, she didn't want to risk disappointing him. No, she wanted to prove that she could give him that control he needed.

With single-minded purpose, he licked through her folds, sucked on her clit, and feasted relentlessly on her swollen flesh, intensifying the liquid heat simmering deep in her core. As his mouth moved on her flesh and his tongue did the most wicked things to her pussy, the morning stubble on his jaw scraped and burned the tender skin on the insides of the thighs framing his face, adding to her sensory overload.

Then his fingers joined in, two of them pushing impossibly deep inside her slick body, then picking up an in-and-out rhythm that matched each breath-stealing stroke of his tongue across that sweet, sensitive spot between her legs. He battered her with sensations, overwhelmed her with the promise of ecstasy. She gasped, and without the use of her hands, she arched her back, trying to press herself closer to that magical mouth—her hips undulating, grinding, as he made her nearly delirious with the need to come.

Another hard, deep thrust of his fingers coupled with the suctioning swirl of his tongue on her clit had her combusting with the force of her orgasm. She cried out his name, thrashing beneath his hold on her hips as the most sublime bliss she'd ever experienced consumed every part of her.

Before she had a chance to come down from that orgasmic high, and even as tiny, climactic aftershocks rippled through her body, Levi quickly moved to a kneeling position between her legs, keeping them spread. Through hooded eyes, she watched as he shoved his cotton shorts down his thighs, releasing his thick, huge erection. For a brief second, she thought he was going to push inside of her, but instead he dragged his fingers through her soaked pussy, coating them with her slick juices. Then he wrapped his lubricated palm tight around his straining dick and stroked the length through his fist.

He pressed his thumb against her still-throbbing clit, rubbing and stimulating that bundle of nerves back to life. She gasped, stunned by the renewed need pulsing low in her belly and the tingling sensation gathering and converging where he was massaging her. Where his gaze was focused on her exposed sex while he pleasured himself at the same time.

She'd never been a part of something so hot and captivating, had never watched a man as he jacked himself off. But she watched Levi now, utterly fascinated by the bold, sexual act. His jaw was clenched, his expression dark and savage as his own desires drove him toward release. His chest heaved, and the muscles along his stomach flexed and bunched as he pumped his engorged shaft through his clenched fist. Each time his cock passed through his grip, the plump head swelled and pre-cum leaked from the tip.

His breathing grew choppy, and he increased the pressure and friction against her clit, pushing her closer to the edge of another soul-baring climax, as well. "*Come again*," he demanded gruffly as he stroked his shaft through his fist, harder, faster.

Shockingly, her body responded to his command,

and she moaned and shuddered as another orgasm surged through her. Even as she was swept up in her own glorious climax, she refused to close her eyes, needing to see Levi succumb to his release.

She met his gaze. The wild intensity glowing in the depths of his eyes was possessive and dominating as he flattened his free hand near her hip and leaned more fully over her, bracing himself for his own orgasm. Another firm pull on his cock and his entire body tensed. She caught the look of pleasure bordering on pain that flashed across his face before he threw his head back, shuddered, and growled hoarsely as he came so hard the initial burst of milky fluid shot all the way up to her breasts and eventually spilled onto her stomach, too.

"Jesus . . . *fuck*," he said on a ragged exhale as he sat back on his heels and tried to catch his breath. When he finally recovered, he took in the mess he'd made all over her, a slow, unmistakable smirk curving the corners of his mouth. His gaze was equally arrogant.

"I'm not gonna lie," he drawled as he slid the tips of his fingers through the sticky substance on her belly, smearing it across her skin. "Seeing my come all over your naked body is hot as fuck." Those same fingers glided through the slippery trail of male essence all the way up to her breasts, where he coated a tight nipple with more of his scent, as if putting his mark on her.

Unable to speak, she merely sighed with pleasure.

"Who knew you were such a dirty girl?" He sounded pleased at the realization.

Before Levi, Sarah never would have guessed that she had a naughty streak in her, but he'd proved her wrong. She'd had sex before, but she'd never been *this* intimate with a man. Or so uninhibited. "It's all your fault," she teased softly.

He grinned unrepentantly. "I'll gladly take the blame for corrupting you."

He moved off the bed, and without an ounce of modesty, he stripped his shorts the rest of the way off, so that he was as naked as she was. He held his hand out to her, and she let him help her to stand, too.

"Come on, dirty girl," he said as he led the way to the adjoining bathroom. "Let's go take a shower and clean you up."

It was an offer she wasn't about to refuse.

Chapter Eight

LEVI RETRIEVED A carton of eggs from the refrigerator, along with some mushrooms, ham, and cheese, to make them each an omelet for breakfast. Sarah was still in the shower—once again, his fault—because as soon as he'd soaped up his hands and begun washing her body, they'd both gotten distracted. Touching Sarah and feeling her soft, wet, naked skin beneath his palms had his dick wanting her all over again, even after his first orgasm should have left him sated. Except he didn't have any condoms in the house—which he planned to rectify today—but that admission hadn't stopped her from going down on her knees in front of him and doing the next best thing.

With her looking up at him with eager blue eyes filled with the desire to please him and warm water from the shower cascading over her shoulders, he knew there was no way he could resist her. Nor did he want to. Was he dying to feel her sweet, soft, innocent mouth sucking him off? Abso-fucking-lutely. But beyond that typical male fantasy, another part of him hoped that their physical connection would be the start to her trusting him with more than just her body. Because there was no denying that Levi wasn't ready to let Sarah go anytime soon, and especially not until he knew whatever she was running from no longer had the ability to harm her in any way.

But all those thoughts fled his mind as he'd leaned against the tile shower stall with his hands tangled in her wet hair, and she'd whispered the words, "Tell me what you want. Show me how you like it best."

In graphic, filthy words that had her wetting her lips in anticipation, he told her all the ways he wanted to fuck her delectable mouth, then watched as she took as much of his cock between those silky lips as she could and proceeded to blow his fucking mind— as well as his dick. She did *everything* he demanded and learned fast as to what he liked the most, even as her own instincts took over.

Her velvet-textured tongue caressed the underside of his shaft, and she gripped the base of his erection tight with her fingers while her lips slid up and down the rigid length of his shaft. And when she reached up and gently massaged his taut balls in her hand, he couldn't stop his eyes from rolling back in pure gratification.

As she continued to work him over, all of her un-certainties vanished, and a sultry vixen took her place as she sucked him like she couldn't get enough of his taste. With each pass, she relaxed a little more, enveloped him a little deeper, and they both moaned when the broad head of his cock finally bumped the back of her throat. She instinctively swallowed around him, squeezing the sensitive tip, and holy fuck, he had to grit his teeth against the blinding jolt of need to unleash the lust pulsing through his cock.

"Goddamn, Sarah. I'm going to come," he warned her in a gruff tone.

She answered him by sucking harder instead of pulling away, destroying him and shredding his control. She closed her eyes, relaxed her jaw, and let him set the pace, even when he anchored his hand at the nape of her neck and started thrusting in earnest as he chased after another orgasm that was no less intense than the one he'd just experienced in the bedroom with her.

The way she'd accepted everything he had to give, and had swallowed every damn drop, had been just as scalding hot as when he'd marked her body with his come. Never had he felt so possessive of a woman as he had with Sarah in that moment, and he'd been shocked by just how much he wanted to claim her and make her his in every way that mattered.

Even now, the recollection was powerful enough to make him shudder all over again and had his unruly dick—which should have been completely drained by those two orgasms—perking up for more.

"Shit," he muttered as he whisked half a dozen eggs into a froth. He could only imagine what it was going to do to him when he finally buried himself in her tight, wet heat and felt her come around his cock.

He exhaled a deep breath and rerouted his thoughts before they made him harder than he already was, especially if he intended to have breakfast ready before Sarah joined him.

Fifteen minutes later, he had two fluffy omelets on a plate, filled with sautéed ham and mushrooms and topped with melted cheese. Just as he finished pouring them each a glass of chilled orange juice, Sarah walked into the kitchen. Her hair was still damp from her shower, and he loved how fresh and natural her face looked ~~without~~ any makeup. She'd put on the same pair of thread-bare jeans that she wore to work that were much too loose on her and an equally old, faded T-shirt. Having helped her pack her belongings last night, he now knew she owned only a few pieces of clothing.

When their gazes met, she gave him a sweet, shy smile, and he knew the pink flush that suffused her cheeks was a result of what she'd just done to him in the shower. She might have been eager to suck his cock, but in the real light of day, she looked so prim and proper and was obviously still coming to terms with how easily she'd relinquished any semblance of modesty with him. While he, on the other hand, intended to coax that naughty behavior out to play every chance he got.

As soon as she reached him, he took her beautiful face in his hands and drew her mouth to his. She came willingly, and as soon as their lips touched, hers automatically parted on a welcoming sigh. He swept his tongue inside, tasting a subtle hint of the mint toothpaste she'd used to brush her teeth as he kissed her softly and slowly, seducing her rather than ravishing her.

Her hands came up to his chest and she melted against him. He loved that she was letting down her walls and trusting him, even if it was just physically for now. He'd take whatever he could get, and hopefully the rest of her would come around in time.

He eventually ended the kiss, and she stared up at him with dreamy eyes hazed over with desire. "Good morning," she murmured.

He skimmed his thumb along her damp bottom lip and gave her a bad-boy grin. "Yeah, it was pretty fucking fabulous."

She caught his sexy reference to the orgasms they'd both enjoyed and ducked her head to hide another rush of color to her face. "Whatever you made smells delicious."

He handed her a plate and a glass of orange juice before picking up his own. "Good, because I expect you to eat every single bite."

"Are you trying to fatten me up?" she asked in a teasing voice as she walked to the dining table and slid into the same chair she'd occupied last night. "Because between the pasta and the chocolate dessert you fed me at dinner, and now this huge omelet, I'm going to gain ten pounds."

"I think we should aim for at least fifteen or twenty," he said seriously as he started in on his own breakfast. While she wasn't malnourished, there was no doubt in his mind that her previous diet hadn't done her body any favors. She was too thin, and he was fairly certain it wasn't by choice.

She picked up her fork but didn't take a bite. "If I'm lucky, it'll go to my breasts and not straight to my stomach and thighs," she said wryly.

"Your breasts are fucking perfect just the way they are." Those soft mounds of flesh had fit into his hands as if they'd been made solely for him, and in his opinion, more than a mouthful was a waste. "If I had any say in the matter, I'd distribute the extra curves to your hips so there's something substantial for me to grab on to when I'm fucking you, and your ass so there's a bit of padding to cushion my hard thrusts when I take you from behind."

Her eyes rounded in shock, and he was satisfied to see that she didn't look opposed to either scenario. Good thing, because that was just barely scraping the surface of all the dirty, sexy things he wanted to do to her.

When she didn't respond verbally, he pointed his fork at her plate. "Now eat, all of it," he ordered like a drill sergeant. "Or I'll put you over my knee and spank you like a bad girl."

Her blonde brows rose, but she didn't seem against that kinky idea, either. Instead, a faint and sassy smile tugged at her lips. "Yes, Officer Kincaid."

And there went his goddamn dick again, twitching at the husky sound of Sarah's voice as she used his rank as a cop in a way that made him envision her in his handcuffs and him as the authority figure. *Oh, fuck yeah.* Tonight, she was going to find out exactly what *Officer Kincaid* was capable of.

After a few minutes of them quietly eating, Levi decided he needed to let Sarah know what he had planned for the day. He glanced across the table as he took a drink of his orange juice, pleased to see she'd finished more than half of her omelet.

"There's some personal things I need to do today that will probably take me a few hours," he said, waiting until she looked up at him before continuing. "I need you to stay in this house and not go anywhere while I'm gone so I don't worry about you, okay?"

She shrugged as she cut another section of her omelet with her fork. "It's not like I have anywhere to go, except to work tonight."

"Good," he said with a nod. "You can spend the rest of the morning and afternoon relaxing and watching TV. I have Netflix, so I'm sure you can find a couple of movies you'd like to see."

She had no idea of his plans, but her job was going to change as of today, because he was done letting Sarah put herself in potentially dangerous situations. For the rest of her time in Chicago, he needed to know that she was in a safe environment, including at her job. But until he talked to Clay and had his brother's agreement, he wasn't ready to inform Sarah of that change to both her place of employment and to her work schedule. He was anticipating an argument when he did, and it was one he intended to win.

"I'll leave my cell phone number with you. If you need anything at all while I'm gone, you call me, okay?"

She took a sip of her juice. "I'm sure I'll be fine."

That wasn't the answer he wanted to hear. He placed his fork on his empty plate, braced his forearms on the table, and made sure she saw his serious-as-hell-expression. "But you'll call me if you need anything, *right?*" he repeated adamantly.

She rolled her eyes at him, as if he were being ridiculous. "Yes, Officer Kincaid."

Oh, yeah, he was definitely bringing out the handcuffs tonight.

THE FIRST STOP Levi made was to the Sleepy Time Motel. Even in broad daylight, the place looked like a fucking shithole, but at least he was there early enough that there weren't any junkies, prostitutes, or drug dealers hanging around yet. He parked his truck and headed toward the front of the motel and the single glass door with a hand-written note taped to the window that read, CHECK IN HERE.

As he stepped inside the tiny office that was more the size of a cubicle with a long, high counter dividing the room into two even smaller sections, a buzzing sound announced his arrival. The office was empty, and when no one appeared to help him, he impatiently pushed the buzzer on the counter until a side door opened and an unkempt, middle-aged man with long, stringy hair and a grungy beard came stumbling out, wearing just a pair of flannel pajama pants.

"Jesus, man," the guy grumbled irritably. "I was on the toilet."

He ambled up to the counter, bringing with him the strong, unpleasant scent of having just smoked weed. The dude looked stoned, but since Levi wasn't here in an official capacity, he didn't give a crap what the guy had been doing before he'd arrived.

"What do you want? Hourly or daily rate?" the man asked as he searched for something beneath the other side of the counter.

"Neither. I'm not here for a room." When the guy narrowed his gaze suspiciously, Levi explained. "You have a guest staying here by the name of Sarah Robins. Room 116. She's been here a few weeks."

Before Levi could finish what he'd been about to say, the other man cut in with an annoyed look. "What's with this chick all of a sudden? Since she's been at the motel, I've never seen her with a john, and now you're the second guy that's come in here asking for her by name."

Levi didn't bother correcting the other guy's assumption. He was too caught up in what the man had just revealed. "What do you mean I'm the *second* guy who's asked about her? When did the other person come by, and what was his name?"

"It was late last night and I don't know what the hell his name was. I didn't ask," he said testily. "I told him her room number, and that's the last I saw of him. It's not my job to keep track of all the johns that stop in here."

Levi's stomach twisted with sudden unease. *Some man had been looking specifically for Sarah*, and he knew damn well it wasn't for the reasons this jerk was insinuating. So, who was the guy and what did he want with her?

"Last night, her room was broken into and she was robbed." Coincidence? Levi had no idea, but he didn't like the fact that the two incidences had happened the same exact evening.

"Yeah, my maintenance guy texted me this morning that the bathroom window was busted open, and when he went inside, the place was trashed." The other guy looked Levi up and down. "You here to pay for the damages, then?"

Levi almost laughed in the man's face. "No. I'm here to *report* the break-in and check Ms. Robins out of this . . . place," he said, catching himself before a more derogatory description fell out of his mouth. "She won't be staying here any longer." Especially now that he knew that another man had come looking for her.

The clerk leaned insolently against the counter. "Yeah, well, if the damages aren't paid for, then *Ms. Robins* can kiss her deposit, and the rest of her week's payment for the room, good-bye."

Levi smiled, and it wasn't a pleasant one. No, this

was an *I'm going to kick your fucking ass and enjoy it* kind of smirk. If the asshole thought it was okay to threaten him, then Levi had no qualms doing the same. It wasn't Sarah's fault that her room had been ransacked, and there was no way in hell Levi was going to let this prick cheat her out of money that was rightfully hers and that she needed now that her stash had been stolen.

Reaching into his pocket, Levi retrieved his wallet and flipped it open to show the pothead his shiny police badge. The guy's eyes widened, and he immediately went pale and took a wobbly step back as an *oh shit* kind of look appeared on his face.

"Yeah, that's right. I'm a cop," he stated, his tone smug because there was no doubt that Levi now had the upper hand in the situation. "Do you really want *me* to file a report with CPD for the break-in and robbery to get Ms. Robin's payment back? Because if I have to take the time to write up a fucking statement, I can guarantee that there will be more than a few other offenses on the report, including *you* being under the influence."

"No, no, of course not," he backtracked quickly, though he didn't look happy about parting with the money. "I'll just write a check for the reimbursement."

No way was Levi accepting a bank check from this dump and risking the chance that it would most likely bounce. "I want it in cash."

The guy's bloodshot eyes glared at him. "I don't have that much money on hand."

"Are you fucking kidding me right now?" Levi boomed incredulously. "Did you not hear me when I said I'm a *cop*? I know that ninety-nine percent of your hourly rate clientele at this hotel pays in cash. Don't dick around with me."

The man's lips pressed into a thin line of annoyance, but he wisely held back the scathing words he undoubtedly wanted to spew at Levi. Instead, he said, "I'll be right back," then disappeared through the side door again.

Levi glanced at the time on his phone, giving the guy five minutes to return before he went and got the goddamn money himself. Luckily, the idiot returned in four and a half and slammed down a handful of dollar bills on the counter in front of Levi.

"See, now that wasn't so difficult, was it?" Levi asked pleasantly after he counted the cash to make sure the guy had included the rest of the week's payment *and* the deposit.

It was all there, so his job here was done, though he couldn't stop wondering about the other man who'd inquired about Sarah. He pocketed the money to give to her when he got back home and smiled at the angry-looking clerk. "Have a nice day," Levi said sarcastically, and headed back to his truck.

One errand down, one to go.

Before leaving the parking lot, Levi texted Clay: *Are you around? I need to talk to you.*

Clay's response came back within seconds. *I'm at the bar doing inventory. Is everything okay?*

It wasn't hard to imagine Clay's worried expression. Old habits died hard for his oldest brother, who'd spent most of his life taking care of, and looking after, Mason and Levi. *Everything is fine. I just need to ask a favor. I'll be there in fifteen minutes.*

Levi drove toward the bar that his brother owned. Kincaid's was located in a more run-down part of the city, and even though Clay had inherited a shitload of money from the previous owner, along *with* the bar, he refused to move the place to a better area. Clay didn't need or want much, but he enjoyed the bar and patrons, though he spent a lot less time there now that he and Samantha were married.

When Levi arrived at Kincaid's, he used the back door to the bar, knowing that it remained open during the early afternoon hours for deliveries. He found Clay in his office, sitting behind his desk and inputting information into his computer. He rapped his knuckles on the doorframe to announce his presence, and his brother glanced up and waved him into the room.

"Hey," Clay greeted as Levi settled into one of the chairs in front of his brother's desk. "How are the fractured ribs?"

"Still sore and bruised," Levi said with a shrug, indulging his brother with the initial small talk. "But nothing I can't deal with."

A wry grin eased across Clay's lips. "You and I both know if that had happened to Mason, he would have been whining to both of us every single fucking day about every little ache and pain."

Levi laughed in agreement, because despite acting tough, their middle brother was far more melodramatic than the two of them had ever been. "That's why I'm the cop, and not him." *Fucking pussy.*

"Speaking of which . . . when do you go back to work?"

"Another two or three weeks, after my doctor clears me for duty again."

Clay raised an inquisitive brow. "Are you bored out of your mind yet?"

Levi had been heading in the direction of boredom, until everything with Sarah had given him something to focus on. "Actually, the past few days have been . . . interesting, and I'm not talking about that ambush of nosey women arriving on my doorstep on Saturday," he said pointedly, because Clay's wife had been a part of that posse of inquisitive females.

Clay chuckled and held up his hands, absolving himself of that decision. "I had nothing to do with it. Mason is on a fact-finding mission about your mystery woman. He's dying to know what's going on between the two of you."

Levi smirked as he stretched his legs out in front of him. "I'm sure he was disappointed when Katrina came home without any top-secret information about Sarah."

His older brother inclined his head to confirm Levi's suspicions, but Clay didn't press for more details, even if his gaze was brimming with curiosity about the woman he'd met at the hospital. Instead, he changed the subject, which really didn't change the direction of the conversation at all since it was all about Sarah.

"So . . . you're not one to ask for favors," Clay finally said as he leaned back in his leather chair and regarded Levi speculatively. "What's up?"

Levi got right to the point. "I need you to hire Sarah as a cocktail waitress at Kincaid's."

Clay's mouth opened, then shut again, clearly taken aback by the unexpected request. And clearly shocked that Levi's *favor* was all about the woman they'd just been discussing.

Finally, after a few quiet moments had passed, his brother spoke.

"Why do you *need* me to hire her?" Clay asked.

His brother didn't hesitate to point out the strong and direct language Levi had used when most people would have asked the question in a more casual manner, like, "*Would you* be able to hire Sarah?" The word *need* implied an emotional connection to Sarah, as well as a personal stake in what happened to her.

And he couldn't deny that he felt *both* of those sentiments.

Clay was waiting for an answer, and Levi knew he owed him an explanation, which would also help his brother to better understand the situation. "For starters, Sarah works at the Circle K where I was shot."

"She was the one who was getting robbed the night you were there, right?" he asked, remembering what Sarah had told him at the hospital.

"Yes. The asshole had a fucking gun pointed to her head," Levi said, uncaring of how protective he sounded. "The mart is also in a shitty part of Englewood, and I'd feel much better if she worked somewhere . . . safe."

"Where you can keep an eye on her?" Clay asked with a raised brow.

"Where she's surrounded by people I *trust*," he clarified. "Also, she's been living in a motel for well over a month, and it's the kind that rents by the hour because that's all she can afford."

Clay winced, his expression immediately sympathetic, because they both knew all about the sacrifices a person had to make when they were scraping every penny to get by. "Jesus."

"And last night, her room was ransacked and robbed," Levi went on so Clay would understand how dire Sarah's situation really was. "Whoever went through the place tore it apart and stole all the money she had. And she didn't have much to begin with."

"And she's still staying there?" Clay asked incredulously.

"Are you fucking kidding me? Of course not." Levi looked Clay in the eye from across the desk, realizing how much he was about to reveal about his personal life—which was something he didn't share openly. Not even with his brothers. It was all part of that control issue of his and learning at an early age to hold everything inside. "Sarah is staying at my place."

Surprise flickered in Clay's eyes, and a lazy smile

kicked up one corner of his mouth. "Damn. And here I thought I was the only one in the family with the White Knight Syndrome."

Levi's brother was known for helping those who were down on their luck in some way, like the damsel in distress he'd rescued, who'd landed in his bar months ago in an attempt to escape marriage to a man she didn't love. Now, that same woman was Clay's wife.

"Don't worry, your nickname, *Saint Clay*, is still intact," Levi assured him with a teasing grin. "Unlike you, I don't make it a habit of rescuing women."

Clay tipped his head curiously. "The fact that you *don't* make it a habit, yet this woman seems to be the exception, is what intrigues me."

Levi had grown up being the one who always analyzed people and situations, and he realized that he didn't like being on the receiving end of his brother's scrutiny. "I'm just trying to help Sarah through a hard time, not marry her," he said sarcastically.

Clay's eyes glimmered with amusement. "Yeah, well, take it from someone who knows firsthand. Helping the *right* woman isn't necessarily a bad thing."

Things had worked out well for Clay, but for as much as Levi was coming to care about Sarah, she'd made it clear that she wasn't staying in Chicago much longer. And while a huge part of him didn't want her to leave, Levi also knew that he had no right to ask her to stay when he'd never been able to sustain a long-term relationship with any woman before. The last thing he wanted to do was lead Sarah on only to break her heart somewhere down the line. None of which meant his stomach wasn't in knots at the thought of her taking off and him never hearing from her again. He'd just have to cross that bridge when he came to it.

Levi also had no desire to elaborate with Clay, so he brought the discussion back to his original purpose for being there at the bar. "You never answered my question. Will you hire her?"

Clay rubbed a hand across his chin as he considered the request once again. "Does she have any experience working in a bar or waitressing?"

"Did Samantha?" he shot right back, reminding his brother that his wife had never worked *any* job before walking into Kincaid's that fateful night.

Levi had no idea if Sarah had ever worked in a bar or a restaurant, but he wasn't about to let Clay use any lack of experience on her part as an excuse not to hire her.

Clay chuckled. "Point taken."

Leaning forward in his chair, Levi braced his forearms on his thighs. "Just give her a chance to prove herself. That's all I'm asking."

"You care about her," Clay murmured. The words were a statement of fact and not a question.

Yeah, Levi cared, probably more than was wise, but he wasn't about to confirm or deny his brother's comment. "Sarah's had a rough life, she's struggling right now, and I just want to make this one thing easy for her."

Clay nodded in understanding, because if there was one thing his brother was very familiar with, it was the hardship and struggle to survive and get by. "Then consider her hired."

Chapter Nine

WHILE LEVI WAS gone, Sarah finished cleaning up the kitchen from breakfast and watched a few shows on TV, keeping an eye on the time since she was scheduled to work tonight and needed to leave in a few hours. If Levi didn't return soon, she was going to have to figure out where the nearest bus stop was so she wasn't late for her shift. He might have insisted that she call him if she needed anything, but she had no idea what errands he was out doing or how important they were, and she didn't want to be an inconvenience.

She'd spent years making it on her own and figuring out ways to improvise in less-than-ideal situations. Lately, her life had become such an upheaval of events, one right after the after, and she was just trying to push through the chaos like she always did. That was one thing she was good at, putting one foot in front of the other despite whatever circumstances or obstacles were set in front of her. And ever since losing her parents, she'd encountered a lot of stumbling blocks, and endured a wealth of heartache, too.

Sarah curled her legs beneath her on Levi's soft couch and released a weary sigh. Not because she was physically exhausted, but emotionally she felt utterly wrung out. She was so tired of struggling every single day, of making wrong choices that led to even more misery. The horrible situation with Dylan being her latest bad decision, all because she'd let down her guard and believed the promises he'd made. Or rather, the lies he'd told her.

And here she was again, falling back into that same familiar pattern with Levi. Yet, even as that thought entered her mind, she had no doubt that he was a man of his word. In the past week alone, he'd proven himself in a multitude of ways, protecting her and keeping her safe when she once again had nowhere else to go and no one else to turn to. He'd asked nothing in return, and no red flags waved in her face. And, if she had to admit the truth, there always were red flags. No, there was no comparing Levi to any of the guys in her past who'd taken advantage of her.

She trusted Levi implicitly, and it scared her just how hard and fast she was falling for him, even as she tried to keep her emotions out of the equation, which was becoming more and more difficult with every passing day. Heck, she'd been fighting her attraction to him since the first day he'd walked into the convenience store and flirted with her. Having spent time with him outside of work, and after everything they'd shared in the past twenty-four hours, she couldn't deny her feelings for him were intensifying quickly.

He was the kindest, most caring and honorable man she'd ever met despite his own damaged past, and even though he was helping her right now and seemed willing to let her stay here with him as long as she needed, she'd learned from experience that nothing this good could last forever. It never did. Something always happened to remind her that she wasn't worthy of being loved, which connected to another deep fear of hers, that she didn't deserve to be happy, not when she'd been the only one to survive the fire that had killed her entire family. Even after all these years, the guilt and grief still had the ability to consume her and fill her with overwhelming sadness.

The sound of someone entering the house from the garage pulled her out of her dismal thoughts. She glanced down the hall just as Levi walked into the kitchen carrying a flat cardboard box and a plastic grocery sack. She moved off the couch to join him, inhaling the delicious, savory scent of the pizza he'd brought home with him, a treat she hadn't enjoyed in way too long. Her mouth watered when he opened the lid and she saw the pepperoni, mushrooms, and gooey cheese toppings.

She took down two plates, realizing how comfortable she already was in Levi's kitchen. In his home.

Don't get used to it, her subconscious taunted, and she quickly squashed the thought before it could depress her.

She handed him one of the plates and took a slice of the pizza. "Why is it that I'm always eating when I'm around you?"

"I'm just contributing to those extra pounds you need to gain," he said, reminding her of their conversation this morning and where he preferred those curves—her hips and butt. "And I figured you hadn't had anything for lunch, so this should hold us through the night so we don't have to worry about dinner."

She was so used to not eating on a regular schedule that skipping meals happened all the time. "I'll definitely have a full belly when I go to work tonight," she said happily.

He looked at her for a long moment as if he wanted to say something, but instead he glanced away and served himself a few pieces of the savory pie. They both leaned against the counter near one another, content to eat their pizza right there in the kitchen.

After a few bites, she broke the easy silence that had settled between them. "Did you get all your errands done?"

"Yes." He held his plate with one hand and reached into the front pocket of his jeans with the other. Withdrawing a small wad of bills, he handed it to her. "This is yours."

Tentatively, she took the money, completely confused. "Mine?" She shook her head and frowned, trying to wrap her mind around how he could have gotten the stolen money back. "Where did you get it?"

"It's not the money that was missing from your room," he said, dispelling that notion. "But I did stop by the motel's office to report the break-in and get you a refund on the rest of your week's payment since you're not staying there any longer."

She stared at him in disbelief. "I'm shocked they gave it back to you."

He shrugged, as if it weren't a big deal. "The guy needed a little motivation to hand over the cash, and I gave it to him."

Setting the money aside, she grinned in amusement, certain she knew what the motivating factor had been. "You flashed your badge and played the big, bad cop, didn't you?"

He chuckled unapologetically. "I might have."

"Well, thank you," she said sincerely. "I appreciate it." It wasn't much money in the scheme of things, certainly not as much as had been stolen, but every dollar made a difference to her and her future.

They finished their pizza, and even though she got the impression that other things were on Levi's mind based on his contemplative expression, he didn't share whatever had him distracted. She helped him wrap up the leftovers in tin foil and put them in the refrigerator. While he took the cardboard box outside to the trash, she set their plates in the dishwasher and wiped down the area, enjoying the domestic chores.

The plastic sack he'd brought in with him earlier was at the far end of the counter, and she grabbed the bag and reached inside to put away whatever he'd bought. She pulled out a black box of Magnum condoms just as she heard Levi walk back into the kitchen.

She glanced up at him with wide eyes and he gave her a sexy grin.

"What's the matter?" he asked, humor lacing his tone as he approached her. "Too presumptuous of me?"

After what had happened this morning between them—in bed and in the shower, she didn't blame him for purchasing the protection. With her staying here under the same roof as him, they both knew that sex was inevitable.

But she raised a brow and couldn't resist teasing him a bit. "Presumptuous because you bought the condoms or because you got the Magnum size?"

His laugh was low and wicked as he pinned her against the counter purposefully, his eyes blazing with heat and desire as he looked down at her parted lips. "Sweetheart, you had your hand wrapped around my hard dick this morning, and as much of it as you could handle in your mouth. Maybe you need a reminder of what you're dealing with?"

The question was more like a salacious dare, and her body responded with a rush of moisture between her thighs. "Yeah, maybe I do."

He dipped his head so his warm breath touched the shell of her ear. "Then let's get you *reacquainted* with the length and width of my dick so there's no doubt in your mind about the size."

Grabbing her hand, he pressed her palm against the fly of his jeans and curled her fingers around the substantial erection already forming. "And since your hand and mouth are having a hard time remembering the exact dimensions of my cock, let's see how it measures up in your tight pussy."

Oh, God. The man's mouth was so filthy, his words so obscene, and it made her hot and wet as hell. She wanted everything he was offering, except the timing couldn't be more wrong. "We can't," she managed, her disappointment clear in her voice. "I have to leave for work soon."

The lust in his gaze cooled a few degrees, enough for her to see the uncompromising glint in his eyes as he looked directly into hers. "You're not going in tonight."

She stiffened against him. What the heck was he talking about? "Of course I am."

"No, you're not," he reiterated, his expression un-flinching. "I made a call to the store manager and told him that you quit."

She gasped, shock rendering her momentarily speechless as she absorbed what he'd just said. She knew he hated where she worked, but she couldn't believe he'd do something so rash that directly affected her livelihood. "Levi, I *need* that job." Panic immediately settled in, and she tried to move away from him.

He grasped her hips, keeping her right where she was. "Calm down, sweetheart," he said in a placating tone. "I promise, you have a job. A new one where you'll be safe and you don't have to worry about some prick pointing a gun at your head again. You'll even make more money than you do at the store."

Her head was spinning as she tried to make sense of what he was saying. "I don't understand."

He smiled, though she didn't miss the cautious look in his eyes as he continued to gauge her reaction. "My brother Clay is hiring you to work at his bar as a cocktail waitress. He pays all his employees way above minimum wage, plus you take home any tips that you make. And he'll give you as many hours as you want or need, and you start *tomorrow* night."

Completely overwhelmed, she stared up at him as the realization of what he'd done sank in. What he'd done *for her*. It was such a thoughtful and kind gesture, and it meant so much to her that it was difficult to hold back the tears threatening to emerge. "Levi—"

He pressed a finger to her lips, cutting her off. "Please don't be mad," he said in a rush, the look in his gaze so caring it made her heart hurt. "I know I should have asked you first, but I didn't want to give you the chance to argue or say no. I can't stand the thought of you working at that store after what happened to you."

His intentions were so good and pure, and she wasn't used to anyone being so selfless on her behalf. "I'm not upset," she said, swallowing back the tightness gathering in her throat. "Actually, I'm very grateful. Thank you."

He exhaled a deep breath, his relief so profound

that the tension in his body eased and he smiled at her again. "It's a good thing you agreed, because I seriously thought I was going to have to get out the handcuffs and use them to keep you here."

She didn't miss the devious look in his gaze, and the thought of being bound by Levi's handcuffs, and letting him have complete control over her pleasure like he had this morning, sent a secret thrill rippling through her. Now that they had all night together, she wanted to take advantage.

Meeting his gaze, she gave him a sultry, inviting smile as she lifted up on her toes and brushed her mouth against his in a tempting kiss. "Go ahead and cuff me, *Officer Kincaid*," she dared in a seductive whisper. "You know you want to."

"*Jesus*," he said on a low, fierce growl that made her shiver with anticipation.

He grabbed one of her hands in his, then picked up the box of *Magnum* condoms she'd set on the counter and led her out of the kitchen. She thought for sure they were headed for his bedroom, but he stopped in the living room in front of the soft, plush couch.

"Stay right here," he ordered, tossing the box of protection onto one of the cushions. "I'll be right back."

She didn't have to wait long for him to return. While in his bedroom, he'd taken off his T-shirt and now only wore his jeans and a wicked-as-sin smile on his gorgeous face. His feet were bare, and a pair of silver shackles dangled from his hand.

Oh, my God, they were really going to do this. She was going to allow this man to restrain her and take her however he desired. And every part of her *wanted* him to.

He stood beside her, his dark green eyes searching hers. "Are you sure you're okay with this?"

She nodded. "Yes."

"Then let's get you undressed." He dropped the cuffs next to the box of condoms, then slid his hands beneath the hem of her T-shirt, pushing the material slowly up her body.

She shivered as his fingers skimmed along her bare flesh, and she raised her arms over her head so he could remove the top. Reaching behind her, he unclasped her bra and let that fall to the floor, too. Her breasts swelled beneath his avid gaze, and she bit back a moan when he tugged her nipples into tight, aching points before trailing his fingers down to the button of her jeans. Leisurely, he unfastened them and lowered the zipper. He shoved the denim down to her thighs, then let her take them the rest of the way off.

That left her in just plain, boring cotton panties, but the way his hungry gaze roved down the length of her made Sarah feel incredibly sexy, and even beautiful.

He picked up the handcuffs and turned back toward her.

"Are those real ones?" she asked curiously. They certainly looked like it.

"Yes. They're my service handcuffs, and I can't wait to see them on you," he said gruffly.

She held out her hands, offering herself to him without hesitation. "Then cuff me, Officer Kincaid," she said huskily. "Make me yours."

MAKE ME YOURS. Sarah's words sparked something hot and possessive in the depths of Levi's stomach and made him realize in that moment just how much he *wanted* this woman to be his. And more than just physically.

It was a crazy thought, considering he'd spent his entire adult life avoiding committed relationships and never investing his emotions when it came to sex, or females in general. But as he looked at Sarah now, standing in front of him vulnerable and nearly naked with her arms extended toward him with such sweet acceptance, something inside of him shifted in a way he'd never experienced before because he'd always been too guarded.

Knowing Sarah's past and her issues with trusting people made this acquiescence of hers all the more humbling, and he saw it for the gift that it was. Her blue eyes were wide and guileless and her body completely relaxed, yielding to him even before he demanded it.

She was fucking perfect for him, in every way.

He'd restrained other women because of his need for control, but Sarah was the polar opposite of every one of those brief, short-lived encounters. She wasn't one of those uncomplicated, mindless fucks he'd sought out in the past, and he refused to treat her the same way. But he wasn't going to lie—the thought of his handcuffs dangling around her delicate wrists made him hard as granite. Restricting her ability to use her hands became all about him heightening *her* pleasure in every way imaginable and not about his own personal hang-ups.

She expected him to secure her hands in front of her, but he did the opposite and drew her arms behind her back, where he proceeded to latch the steel loops around her small wrists. He made sure they weren't too tight, then couldn't resist caressing a finger slowly down the indentation of her spine. She shivered, and the soft, delightful moan she released went straight to his already pulsing dick.

She turned her head and tried to look at him. "Is this where you get to frisk me?" she asked breathlessly, playfully.

He smiled. "You want to be frisked?"

She nodded her head. "Yes, please, Officer Kincaid."

Still standing behind her, he hooked his thumbs into the waistband of her panties and pushed them down her legs until they dropped to her feet. Moving closer to her backside, he nudged his knee between her thighs. "Spread these gorgeous legs for me, dirty girl. I want to make sure I do a very *thorough* search."

She widened her stance, then sucked in a quick

breath when he reached around and took her breasts in his hands, fondling them and lightly pinching her nipples.

"What are you hoping to find?" she asked oh-so-innocently.

"A soaking-wet pussy," he breathed into her ear as his splayed hands slid down her stomach toward his destination. "It's my job to make sure that this body is ready to be fucked, Magnum style."

She laughed softly, then moaned when his fingers delved into her soft folds of flesh, already slick with desire. "Am I wet enough for you?"

"Not yet." He bit the bare curve of her neck, drawing a startled gasp from her that made him smile. "But you will be after I make you come."

He released her and stepped away, and she made a sound of protest at the loss of his touch.

"Don't worry, sweetheart," he said as he walked around in front of her and gently trailed the backs of his fingers along her flushed cheek. "I'm not going to leave you hanging for long."

Initially, he'd had every intention of bending her over the couch so he could drive into her from behind, hard and deep, but he quickly changed his mind because everything about being with Sarah was different. *She* was different, and when he pushed his cock into her this first time, he wanted to see her face as her tight pussy gradually stretched to accommodate all of him. He wanted to watch as she unraveled just for him and wanted to feel her internal muscles clench around him as she came all over every inch of his shaft, right before he let go of his own release.

He quickly shucked his jeans and briefs, then sat down on the sofa in front of where Sarah was still standing. Her glazed eyes took in the hard, thick length of his erection as he tore open a condom and sheathed himself. She licked her lips, and as much as he'd love to have her delectable mouth on him again, he wanted deep inside her more.

"Come here and straddle me," he ordered softly, and when she stepped forward, he grabbed her waist and helped her to kneel above his lap. She started to lower herself, but he shook his head and kept her poised above his thighs.

"Not yet," he said, smoothing his hands down her hips and along the creases of her thighs, until his thumbs were spreading her pussy open so he could see all the pretty folds in between. "I want you wetter than you already are so you can take all of me."

He pushed two long fingers inside of her, rubbed his thumb against her swollen, needy clit, and she dropped her head back on a shuddering moan. He continued to stroke her, slow and deep, enjoying the front-row seat he had to watch her uninhibited response to every seductive touch, every intimate caress that brought her closer and closer to where he needed her to be. With her hands cuffed behind her back and her knees braced apart, there wasn't much she could do except rock her hips back and forth and ride his hand in an attempt to chase her elusive release.

His dick twitched impatiently, and then he finally felt what he'd been waiting for . . . the fluttering sensation around his fingers, the fresh rush of moisture that coated his hand, and the inarticulate sounds she made as an orgasm started to roll through her.

An orgasm that belonged to *him*. He wanted it. Needed to be a part of it, and a part of her. Knowing he had to act fast, he pulled out his fingers, aligned the head of his cock to the entrance of her body, then took hold of her waist and pulled her down hard at the same time he bucked his hips upward, burying himself to the hilt. She cried out at the initial deep, endless thrust that filled her completely and literally stole his breath from his lungs.

And before he could recover, his sweet, sexy, beautiful Sarah went wild on him, her pretty breasts bouncing enticingly as she slid up and down his throbbing shaft in jerky movements. Her thighs clenched against his as she undulated her hips while grinding her pussy hard against his pubic bone for added friction, for both of them.

It was all too much. Sensory fucking overload.

Belatedly, Levi realized why he didn't normally care for this position, why he'd always avoided it in other encounters. Because despite Sarah having her hands restrained, she was still able to strip him of control, and for the first time in his life, he didn't try and take it back. He let her have it. He fucking encouraged her to *take it*.

He tunneled his fingers into her hair, cupping the

back of her head and forcing her dark blue gaze to meet his. "Fuck me, Sarah," he commanded gruffly. "However you want. Whatever it takes to make you come."

She whimpered as she moved more rhythmically on top of him, then leaned into him and brought her lips close to his. "Kiss me, Levi," she said, her voice ragged with need.

Tightening his fingers in those silky strands, he slanted his mouth across hers. She welcomed the thrust of his tongue, sucking on it and making him groan low in his throat. Perspiration slickened their bodies as they strained against one another, but it still wasn't close enough. Hard enough. Deep enough.

He feared it never would be.

He released her hair and grabbed her ass in his hands, hauling her forward in a way that scraped across her clit and made her entire body quake. Desire, lust, and need collided inside of him, sending Levi over the edge as Sarah's inner walls gripped him tight, squeezing every ounce of pleasure out of him and milking his cock until he had nothing left to give. Until he knew he'd never be the same.

Sarah had no idea, but she fucking *owned* him.

Chapter Ten

WITH SARAH COLLAPSED against his chest, her body lax, and her breathing gradually returning to normal after what had just happened between them, Levi wrapped an arm around her waist and managed to reach down to the floor and grab his jeans without letting her fall off his lap.

She barely moved, testament to just how spent she was, and it made him smile. *She* made him smile. Somehow, and in a very short time, she'd managed to make him feel things he'd never allowed to slip past the walls he'd built around his heart . . . hope, need, and an unfamiliar yearning that was startling in its intensity. Shockingly, he didn't fight the sensations. No, for the first time in his life, he welcomed them, even realizing that, in the end, she could still walk away—but he'd make it damn difficult for her to do so when or if the time came.

He managed to retrieve the key from the front

pocket of his pants, and he released Sarah's wrists from confinement. Her arms flopped to her sides, and he chuckled as he massaged them just in case they'd fallen asleep. Hell, he was beginning to think that *she'd* fallen asleep.

He stroked his hands up and down her back. "Hey. You still with me?"

"Barely," she murmured, her warm breath caressing his neck before she slowly lifted her head and met his gaze. "What just happened?"

He chuckled. She looked dazed and bewildered, in the best way possible, and he couldn't resist teasing her. "I think you just got well acquainted with a Magnum-sized cock."

An adorable blush swept across her cheeks, even as she rolled her eyes at him. "Yeah, that might take some getting used to," she said with a cute little smirk. "Not that I'm complaining, because you felt pretty damn amazing."

"It was all you, sweetheart," he said, enjoying this lighthearted banter between them that felt so easy and natural. "I need to go and clean up. How about you stay here and I'll be right back?"

"Okay," she said, and crawled over to the long section of the couch where she could still lie down.

He stood up and covered her with the lightweight blanket he kept folded over the sofa, then disappeared into the bathroom. He returned a few minutes later, still naked, and settled beneath the covers next to her. She immediately snuggled against him, so warm and soft and content, and he realized for the first time ever that the couch was a great place to cuddle.

Wait. Had the word *cuddle* seriously just entered his vocabulary? *Yes, yes, it had,* and Jesus, Mason would have a field day with that one.

Mentally shaking his head, Levi tucked Sarah into the crook of his arm, wanting to keep her just like this, safe and secure so nothing could ever hurt her. At least she was no longer working at the Circle K in a shitty neighborhood, but he couldn't stop thinking about what the motel clerk had said to him earlier today about some guy asking about Sarah.

"Can I ask you something?" Sarah said, taking the words right out of his mouth before he could ask her what was on *his* mind.

"Sure." He absently caressed his hand down her bare arm, figuring he'd answer her question first, then he she'd owe him in return. "You can ask me anything."

"Anything?" She lifted her head and grinned at him, her eyes sparkling playfully. "You sure about that?"

He hesitated before replying. He had no idea what she wanted to know, but he was shocked to realize that he truly didn't mind sharing things about himself with her. Maybe because she'd grown up similarly and had a past as painful as his own, it made it easier for him to open up to her. He knew there wouldn't be any judgment, just understanding.

"Yeah, I'm sure. What's on your mind?"

"I really enjoyed what we just did," she said with a genuine smile, though he didn't miss the tentative note to her voice. "And I know putting the cuffs on me is all tied into that issue of you being in control, and you've been very clear about that up front. But you said something last night while we were eating dinner that I keep thinking about."

"And what's that?" They'd discussed a lot of things last night, mainly her past, while he'd been far vaguer about his. At the time, that had been a deliberate tactic on his end.

Her index finger absently traced imaginary patterns on his chest, and her brows knit into a pondering frown. "You made a comment about when you were a little boy, how you were always being threatened to be good or you'd be taken away. Who did that to you?"

He exhaled a deep breath and glanced away from her inquisitive gaze. He'd known a personal question had been looming, but he never would have guessed that she'd ask about the most difficult part of his childhood. The one that had shaped and molded him in ways that had affected every aspect of his life because of the dark, ugly secrets he'd been forced to carry and the emotions he'd had to stifle in order to survive.

He'd been five years old at the time, but now he was a grown man. The devastating, frightening threat his junkie mother had issued couldn't hurt him any longer. He'd always tried to keep that part of his past buried deep—*no one* knew what he'd endured, not even his brothers, because his mother had used them as part of her intimidation, as well. Maybe it was time to let it all out, so he could release the anger and bitterness tied to those memories.

When he remained quiet for too long, she laid her head back down on his shoulder. "If you don't want to talk about it, I understand," she said softly.

"I *do* want to talk about it, at least with you." The words came out before he could think twice about it, but he didn't regret them. "But I have to warn you up front, it's not a pretty story."

He felt her smile against his chest. "You and I have that in common. Neither one of us had a simple or idyllic childhood, so I doubt anything you say would shock me."

He wasn't so sure about that, but as he threaded his fingers through her soft hair, he decided to be completely honest about everything. "You already know about my mother being a junkie and a prostitute. Drugs were all she cared about, and as far back as I remember, up until the age of five, while my brothers were in school she'd take me with her on what she'd called her 'special errands.' She didn't want to leave me alone in our apartment and risk someone calling social services, but *fuck*, I really wish she'd left me behind."

She looked back up at him, her expression pained. "How bad was it?"

"*Really* bad," he said, his voice already feeling raw, his stomach in knots. "First, she had to get money for her drugs, and we'd end up in dark alleys that scared the shit out of me. And she wasn't particular about how she made that cash. She'd make me sit in the backseat of her crappy car while she'd give any random john a blow job in the front seat, or she'd make me wait all alone in the vehicle while she disappeared into a seedy motel room for an hour in a drug-infested neighborhood where anyone could have taken me. *I was five fucking years old,*" he said, his entire body vibrating with anger.

She wrapped her arms tight around him, hugging him in a way he'd never been held before. Like a solid anchor in this turbulent sea of emotions he was navigating. Physically, he felt her comfort and support, but she remained quiet, giving him the chance to purge every last repulsive recollection.

"I remember men coming up to the car while she was gone and trying to lure me out with candy or a promise of a toy." Pedophiles, most likely, Levi knew now. "I'd keep the windows up and the doors locked because I was so terrified, but sometimes it was so damn hot that I'd be drenched with sweat by the time she got back into the car. By then she had the cash she needed, and all that mattered to her was buying that little bag of crack or meth or heroine. She didn't care which. And once she had it, she didn't hesitate to snort the powder or shoot up right in front of me."

He could hear the disgust in his voice, could feel the clench of his jaw as he relived that nightmare. "There were so many times I cried and begged her not to take me, to leave me home. I told her how afraid I was, and there were a few times when I even had a panic attack, but she didn't care. And then I made the mistake of telling her that I was going to tell Clay about her 'errands,' and she completely flipped out on me and went into a rage. She told me to shut the fuck up, that if I said anything to anyone about where we went or what she did, I'd be taken away. I'd never see Mason or Clay ever again."

The heartless bitch had played on his worst fears as a kid, because his older brothers were everything to him, and the only two people in his life he cared about and he knew would make him feel safe. But his own mother had denied him that sense of security. She'd forced him to endure her sordid lifestyle and keep her secrets because he'd been terrified of losing Clay and Mason, of never seeing them again.

Beside him, Sarah had stiffened, her body language letting him know that, yeah, he'd shocked her, after all. And when she lifted her head once again, the pain shimmering in her eyes made his heart tighten in his chest.

"So, in order to cope and control your fears, you shut down in the only way you knew how," she said.

He realized *why* she understood him so well. Probably because she'd done the same thing after that foster family had left her behind. "Yeah. I had to stuff all those emotions deep inside and keep them buried. It all ended when I was finally old enough to go to school at the same time as my brothers, but when my mother passed away when I was eight, everything changed drastically once again."

"That's when your brother Clay started raising you and Mason, right?" she asked, remembering some of the details he'd shared with her.

He nodded. "Yes. And since Clay was always worrying that we'd be separated or taken away if social services ever found out about our situation, he'd always tell me and Mason that we needed to be good and stay out of trouble and not say a word to anyone about our situation. Behaving and doing what Clay said was easy for me, because by then I'd already learned how to control my emotions and keep everything inside. I was straight-laced and disciplined, which was a good thing since Mason was constantly testing Clay's patience and authority."

She reached up and touched his cheek, her fingers warm and soft and soothing. "I'm so sorry you had to go through all that."

He shrugged and gently grabbed her hand, placing it back on his chest, right over his beating heart. "Last night, when I took you back to the motel, it reminded me of the places my mother would take me, and it made me physically ill to think of you staying there." Which reminded him . . . "By the way, when I was getting your money back today, the front desk clerk mentioned that some guy had been asking around about you. He wanted your room number, and the asshole gave it to him without getting *his* name. Not sure if this guy is connected to the break-in, but would you happen to know who this person might be?"

With every word he spoke, Sarah's eyes got bigger and bigger. He saw panic and fear collide in the depths as she stared up at him and whispered, "Oh, God," in a strangled voice. "What if I'd been there last night?"

She abruptly sat up, holding the blanket to her chest as she tried to move away from him. He quickly scrambled upright, too, and caught her arm, refusing to let her go until he had some answers because something was wrong. *Very* wrong.

"Sarah?" Her name was a soft demand for her attention, to snap her out of her haze of distress, but it didn't seem to work. "Who was it?"

Her face was pale, her breathing labored as she ran a trembling hand through her hair. "I knew it was just a matter of time," she mumbled, more to herself than him.

"Before what?" he asked impatiently, wanting to shake the answers out of her but trying like hell not to spook her further.

She turned dread-filled eyes to him. "Before he found me."

Jesus Christ. Someone was stalking her, Levi realized, and felt as though he'd been punched in the gut. "Who, Sarah?" He clasped her hand in his, trying not to roar in frustration. "Before *who* found you?"

"My ex," she finally revealed in a small voice. "A guy I'd been dating for a few months."

And with that revelation, so many other things now made sense to Levi. Where she'd worked, the off-the-beaten-path motel she'd been staying at, the cash she'd kept on hand, and her insistence that she was leaving Chicago. His intuition had been right, and he was relieved that he had a few answers, though he suspected there was a lot more she needed to tell him. It didn't seem as simple as a bad breakup with an ex-boyfriend.

He forced himself to relax, hoping it would calm her down, as well. He sat back on the couch and drew her to him. "Come here," he said gently, and guided her so she was sitting sideways on his lap. She now had all of the blanket wrapped around her body, which was a good thing considering they were both still naked and it would be a helluva distraction having her ass pressed against his dick.

She was staring straight ahead, her vulnerable expression revealing all of her worries. He touched her chin and turned her face toward his so she was looking at him. "You need to tell me what's going on. Straight up, Sarah. No more evading my questions or making excuses." He needed facts and details in order to help her and understand what he was up against. "Are you running from this guy?"

"Yes," she said in a barely audible voice.

He'd expected as much, but hearing her confirm it made his protective instincts skyrocket into overdrive. "Tell me why."

She shook her head stubbornly. "This isn't your problem."

He knew she was used to being alone and handling things by herself, but there was no way he was going to let any other man put his hands on her. Ever. "Sweetheart, I'm making it my problem. As of right now. You're going to start at the beginning, and you're going to tell me everything. All of it."

He could see her reluctance, but she finally spoke. "His name is Dylan Harper. I met him a few months ago when I was waitressing at a diner. He'd come in every day for coffee and a piece of pie, and he always sat in my section. He seemed like a nice guy, so when he asked me out, I said yes."

She picked at a piece of lint on the blanket, averting her gaze as she continued. "We dated for about a month, then one day he told me we were going to a friend's place for a barbeque about an hour and a half away from Chicago in Fairdale. It was a rural area, in the middle of nowhere. It was this small gated community called Sacrosanct, which Dylan told me meant *blessed*. When we arrived, the only reason we gained entrance was because of a tattoo on the inside of Dylan's wrist that he showed the guy at the security gate. I thought that was odd, but once we were inside, everything seemed normal. At first."

She stopped talking, and Levi gently brushed a few strands of hair from her cheek and prompted her to continue. "What do you mean, at first?"

"There was this huge main house that was beautifully maintained, and around it were clusters of smaller cabins where other people lived. Well over a hundred, I later found out. The community was fully sustainable, with fields of organic fruits and vegetables, a stable of pigs and cows and chickens, and well water. Everything ran on solar power, so nobody had to leave for anything, but I didn't realize the implications of any of that until I was ready to go, and Dylan told me that this was our new home."

Levi's gut twisted with unease. "Couldn't you just leave?"

"I thought I could," she said quietly as she pulled the blanket tighter around her body. "But the main gate was always locked with a guard who had strict orders on who could come and go, and there was a ten-foot-high block fence around the entire community. It didn't take me long to realize that this place was a cult, and I was being held against my will."

Shit. He could feel and hear how difficult this was for her to talk about, but he continued to encourage her to go on, to tell the story however she needed to. "What happened?"

She swallowed hard. "I was placed in a cabin with three other women who were ordered to watch over me, and I had to attend daily rituals where the leader of the group, an older man named Rick, brainwashed members into worshiping him as a holistic being. While everyone seemed in awe of him, I was the only one who had a problem handing over my loyalty, dependency, and trust to a man who controlled everything and everyone in the community."

Her bare legs were peeking out of the covers, and he gently trailed his hand along one of them. "How long were you there?"

"Three weeks." She met his gaze, and he hated how ashamed she looked, as if it had somehow been her fault that she'd been trapped there. "I fell into line with the others, only because I knew it would be the only way for anyone to believe that I'd been converted into being a follower and I'd be able to walk around the place more freely. I also saw a possessive, threatening side to Dylan that scared me, and he made it clear that if I ever tried to leave or escape, he'd find me and bring me back. Deserting the Sacrosanct community is considered a punishable offense, but I was desperate to get out of there."

Obviously, she'd escaped, and he couldn't imagine how she'd gotten through such a well-guarded place. When she remained silent, he nudged her once again with words. "What did you do?"

"Every day, I tried to look for a way to get out of there, and after three weeks, I noticed at the far end of the secured grounds that there was a thick tree limb overhanging the block wall into the compound, and I knew that was my only hope of escaping. It took me a few days of thinking, but I ended up getting a long line of rope and I threw it over the limb, then used it to help me climb up the wall with my feet until I could grab the top and go over it."

"That's pretty damned resourceful," he said, impressed that she'd figured out a way to utilize the branch.

"I was desperate," she said with a small shrug. "I had a few things in my backpack and fifty dollars in my pocket that I stole from the main house. I hitch-hiked my way back to Chicago and had to live on the streets for a while until I could find a job and a place I could afford to live . . . I still feel so stupid and naive for getting myself into such a bad situation."

"Sweetheart, it's not your fault," he said, trying to soothe her. "All that matters is that you're out now. You're here with me now and you're safe. I'm not going to let anything happen to you."

She lifted tear-filled eyes to him, which nearly shattered his heart. "You can't make a promise like that. If Dylan tracked me to the motel, he'll find me again." A shudder racked her body. "And if he gets me back into the compound, I'll never be free again."

"If he does find you, I can *guarantee* that he won't hurt you," he said fiercely.

She shook her head in denial. "You can't protect me forever."

Yes, he could. He caught her chin in between his fingers so she was looking into his eyes. He understood that he couldn't keep her locked up in his house indefinitely, but Levi could keep her safe until *he* could find this asshole himself and make sure he never touched Sarah again. As a cop, he had resources, and in this instance, he had no problems taking advantage of that support.

"Listen to me," he said, determined to reassure her, to ease the panic reflected in her eyes. "You'll be working at my brother's bar, surrounded by people I trust who are like family to me and my brothers. Clay will make sure that everyone knows about Dylan, and you won't ever be alone. I'll take you to Kincaid's and pick you up, and if I can't be with you, someone I trust will be. Always." And *that* was a vow he wouldn't break.

"Just until I can save enough and leave," she insisted, compromising in the only way she would allow. "I don't want to be a burden and inconvenience, to you or anyone else."

She was neither to him. In fact, she'd become so much more than what he'd ever anticipated, all in a very short amount of time. But it had become increasingly clear that Sarah *believed* she was a nuisance because that's how she'd been treated since her parents' deaths. Right now, in this moment, there was no convincing her otherwise. For now, it had to be enough that she trusted him, and Levi refused to give her any reason to regret that choice, or do anything to disappoint her like so many other people in her life had.

"Let's just take everything one day at a time, okay?" he asked so she didn't feel pressured to make impulsive decisions based on her unstable emotions right now.

"Okay," she said softly, her expression weary.

Satisfied that she'd agreed, he pushed his fingers into her hair at the side of her face and brought her head to his shoulder. He glided his thumb across her soft cheek, and she let out a sigh and snuggled closer. Gradually, her body relaxed against his, and he felt her steady, even breaths against the side of his neck and knew that she'd fallen asleep.

He held her for a while, thinking about their conversation while trying to set up a plan in his mind. She was right . . . Dylan sounded like the kind of guy who wasn't going to give up, which meant Levi needed to be proactive when it came to finding the asshole before he tracked Sarah down again. It wouldn't be easy considering he didn't have much information on the guy, and the compound in Fairdale wasn't in his jurisdiction as a cop, but that wouldn't stop him from digging up what he could on her ex.

LEVI WAITED UNTIL later that night when Sarah was asleep in his bed, then grabbed his cell phone and went into the kitchen to make a call.

His partner, Nick, picked up on the second ring. "Hey, Ironman! What's up?"

"I need to ask a favor," he said, skipping any idle chitchat and getting right to the point of the call.

"Anything," Nick replied, immediately on board.

"It has to do with Sarah."

"Sarah, the woman from the convenience store?" Nick asked, his tone incredulous.

"Yeah, that Sarah." As if there was any other in his life. But Nick wasn't aware of everything that had happened between Levi and Sarah since he'd gotten shot, so he understood his partner's surprise.

"Damn. Did you finally get lucky?" Nick joked.

"Actually, she did agree to a date with me," Levi said, but didn't elaborate, not when there were more pressing matters to discuss. Instead, he filled Nick in on what had happened after the date, when he'd taken Sarah back to the motel, and her confession tonight about being stalked by a controlling, possessive ex who was a member of a cult.

"You know we don't have any authority if he's living in Fairdale," Nick replied once he had all the facts. "That's out of our jurisdiction."

"Yeah." He rubbed his fingers across his forehead, trying to ease the tension settling there. "What I need is as much information about this guy as you can get for me. His name is Dylan Harper, and all I know is that he's currently living at the Sacrosanct compound. I want to pay him a friendly visit as a civilian to make sure he doesn't do anything stupid, if you know what I mean." There wouldn't be a physical confrontation that jeopardized his job as a cop, but verbally, Levi planned to be *very* persuasive.

"Oh, yeah, I know exactly what you mean," Nick said, a smirk in his voice. "I'll see what I can find out about him this week and get back to you."

"Perfect. Thank you."

Levi disconnected the call, feeling marginally better. Now that he had Nick digging up whatever he could on Dylan, tomorrow Levi planned to make sure that both Clay and Mason were apprised of the situation before Sarah started her shift at Kincaid's later that night. He wanted protective eyes on her at all times. If for some reason Levi couldn't be there, then he knew his brothers would provide backup until the issue with Dylan was resolved and Sarah no longer had a reason to run. At least, that's what Levi was hoping.

Hearing the familiar padding of footsteps on the wood flooring, he glanced up as Sarah walked into the kitchen, looking drowsy, a little disheveled, and sexy as hell in one of his navy blue Chicago PD T-shirts.

"What are you still doing up?" she asked, her voice husky as she walked straight to him and wrapped her arms around his waist as if it was the most natural thing in the world. "I don't like waking up alone."

He didn't know if it was her sleepy subconscious talking or an honest declaration, but he loved that she'd missed him enough to seek him out. "Just taking care of a few things." *Taking care of you.*

"Come back to bed," she whispered.

It was an invitation he couldn't refuse, even if it was just to hold her while she slept.

Chapter Eleven

"WHAT SIZE JEANS do you wear?"

Sarah followed Samantha through the women's section of Target, with Katrina trailing behind. Levi had surprised her this morning with the announcement that the two of them were having lunch with Clay and his wife, Samantha, and Mason and his fiancée, Katrina. While eating their meal at an Italian restaurant near Clay's bar, Sarah mentioned to the women that she needed to buy jeans for her shift at Kincaid's later that evening, and they'd both insisted on coming with her.

"Last time I bought a pair, they were a size five," she said as they came to a wall with shelves that held folded pairs of jeans. Samantha went right for the darker pairs and started looking through the pile.

Katrina stopped at a rack of cute dresses and glanced through them while Sarah gravitated toward a nearby clearance rack to see if she could find anything there. The two women had been so nice to her, and right from the moment she'd met Samantha, she'd noticed that she was the nurturing type. She was also stunningly beautiful and well put together in a polished, sophisticated way. But she looked right at home in Target, and she seemed to know where everything was located.

Sarah had never had close girlfriends growing up because of being shuffled through so many foster homes and her fears of getting attached, only to leave people behind. Or them leaving *her* behind. Even as an adult, she didn't have any close friends, so having this girl time with Samantha and Katrina was a nice change. And fun, too. She'd laughed so much during their lunch and already felt a friendship forming, even if it was just for a short while.

"The men over there look like they're having such a deep, important conversation," Katrina said, her tone amused. "But man, do they look damn hot all standing together."

Sarah glanced over her shoulder, and sure enough, Levi, Mason, and Clay were in a tight circle in the aisle that separated the women's section from the men's, and yeah, she agreed that all three men were good-looking in their own separate ways. Their arms were crossed over their chests, and all of their expressions were serious as the two older brothers listened to whatever Levi was saying to them.

"They're either being serious about something or annoying one another. I'm not sure which," Samantha said with a grin.

Sarah had a feeling they were talking about *her*. Levi told her that lunch today with his siblings and their significant others was so that she could meet everyone before starting her shift tonight, but she suspected that Levi was letting his brothers know about Dylan. Levi was determined to keep her safe—hence his insistence that he accompany her to Target, which then prompted Samantha and Katrina to join them. Sarah really did appreciate his efforts and knew he'd do his best. But she'd meant what she said when she'd told him that he wouldn't be able to protect her forever from someone who was highly motivated to find her.

"You know, I have to say, I've never seen Levi so smitten with a woman as he seems to be with you," Samantha said as she pulled a folded pair of jeans from a stack and straightened with the pants in her hands.

"To be honest, we've never seen him with a woman at all," Katrina added with a grin. "So you must be very special to him."

Sarah couldn't stop the warm blush that crept up her neck and over her face. The fact that Levi had never brought a girlfriend around to meet his family and friends was surprising and shocking. But even knowing she was an exception—which she attributed directly to her situation with Dylan and not having a place to live—she refused to read too much into their comments.

"So, Mason and I are getting married next month in an outdoor ceremony at Clay and Samantha's house," Katrina said off-handedly. "Levi already RSVP'd just for himself *before* you started dating, but I hope you'll come, too?"

Sarah *really* liked these two women. A lot. And she knew they were trying to make her feel welcome and a part of a group. But chances were that, in a month, she'd be gone. "Thank you for the invitation. I appreciate it," she said, but didn't give Katrina a firm response.

"Here's a pair of jeans in your size," Samantha said triumphantly, just as Sarah found one on clearance.

She pulled the denim from her rack as she reached for the pair Samantha held out to her. She'd try both of them on, but with her limited funds, Sarah was hoping the cheaper pair fit better, because there was no way she was letting Levi pay for anything.

While Katrina continued perusing other outfits, Samantha walked with Sarah to the dressing room. Before they reached the counter, she lightly touched Sarah's arm and brought her to a stop. She glanced at the other woman curiously, not sure what she wanted or needed.

Samantha's gaze was kind and genuinely caring. "I hope you don't mind, but Clay told me a bit about what you've been through lately. Being held up at the mart, then having your room broken into and trashed . . . I'm really very sorry, and if there is anything I can do to help you out, don't ever hesitate to ask." Then she smiled sweetly. "I've had a similar experience in starting over with nothing, so I understand how hard it can be."

Sarah blinked at Samantha, stunned by her offer of help but also shocked that this gorgeous, refined woman could relate to her situation. "Thank you."

Samantha hesitated for a moment, then decided to speak whatever was on her mind. "I also wanted to tell you that Levi is a great guy, and he's the real deal, just in case you haven't already figured that out for yourself."

"I have," she assured the other woman. But none of this was about Levi or how great of a guy he was. It was about Sarah's messed up life and the fact that she couldn't offer Levi even one tenth of what he was giving to her.

Samantha gave her one last smile, along with a gentle arm squeeze, then headed back toward where the guys were standing. Sarah went into her assigned dressing room, her mind spinning with everything that Samantha had just told her.

She already knew that Levi was a one-of-a-kind guy—that had been evident since the first day she'd met him at the convenience store. But what she'd learned about him over the past few days had only solidified that impression. She'd never come across a man so genuine and caring and protective. Or one with a childhood as tragic as her own.

As she took off her old, faded jeans, she thought about everything that had transpired last night. The way he'd opened up to her about his mother had nearly broken her heart, but what really got to her was the way he'd listened while she'd told him about Dylan and how quickly he'd come to her defense without judging her at all.

Levi was everything she could ever want in a man, but she'd learned time after time that anything good in her life never lasted long. If there was any real happiness for her to find, it was always stolen away right when she became too complacent. When something started to feel too good to be true, it usually was, and heartache ensued. It was a cycle she couldn't seem to escape, so why would Levi be any different?

It didn't matter that she was seriously falling for him, she thought as she put on the less expensive jeans and looked at herself in the mirror—grateful to see that they fit just fine. It didn't matter that sex with him was like nothing she'd ever experienced before—and probably never would again. And it definitely didn't matter that he made her happy and hopeful and so incredibly content when she was with him. No, that was usually the warning sign that, just around the corner, life was going to pull the rug out from under her feet. Again.

So, for right now, she just needed to be grateful for the time she had with him and enjoy every moment—even as a huge lump formed in her throat at the thought of her time with Levi coming to an end.

She forced back the emotion and stripped off the pair of jeans just as she heard a male voice talking to the dressing room attendant. A moment later, a knock sounded on her door, startling her.

"Hey, did you find a pair of jeans that worked?" Levi asked in a low voice.

The corner of her mouth kicked up in a smile, the same way her heart raced a little faster whenever he was around, and she welcomed the distraction from her too depressing thoughts. Unlatching the door, she stood behind it since she was only dressed in a shirt and her underwear, and peered out at him. "Yes, I found a pair. What are you doing in the women's dressing room and how did you get in here?"

He gave her a sinful smile that immediately made her melt inside. "I thought you might need some help, or my opinion about how they fit." He lowered his voice and winked at her. "At least, that's what I told the girl out there."

"I already took them off," she said, not trusting that smile or devilish wink for a second.

"Even better," he murmured, and easily pushed his way inside the room.

She was too astonished by his bold move to do anything but gape at him and step back as he entered. The moment he closed and locked the door, then backed her up against the nearest wall, she knew she was in trouble. The sexy kind of trouble she knew would be difficult to resist.

Before he got any closer and obliterated her ability to think, she pressed both palms against his chest to stop his approach. He halted, even though she knew her hand was no real deterrent for what he had in mind. "Where are the girls?" she whispered. "And

Mason and Clay?" The thought of them waiting outside of the dressing room while Levi did . . . whatever he intended to do, make her cheeks warm.

"I told them that I could handle things from here, so they left." He gently grabbed the hands she'd planted on his chest, raised them both above her head, and easily secured them against the wall with one of his own. Then he wedged his knee between her legs, forcing them a few inches apart.

Her eyes widened and her pulse hammered, in panic *and* excitement, when she realized his intent. "You wouldn't dare!" she said in a low, hissing voice.

"Yeah, I would," he replied unabashedly, and followed up that promise by slipping his fingers into the waistband of her panties. "Consider it another one of my fantasies I didn't know I had until right this very moment. The thought of giving you an orgasm in a public place is making me hot as fuck."

His fingers slid directly between her thighs and into her pussy, making her suck in a gasp as he concentrated his efforts on her clit, bringing it to life with a few skillful strokes. Immediately, she knew this wasn't going to be a slow and leisurely climb. No, it was going to be fast and reckless and wild.

She bit back a moan when he pushed two fingers deep inside and rubbed his thumb over that bundle of nerves, drawing more moisture from her body. The wicked grin he gave her said it all—that he knew how aroused she already was, and he was thoroughly enjoying himself despite the pleasure being all hers.

She tried to bring her hands down to grab his head to kiss him, to smother the noises she was trying desperately not to make, which would draw attention to their room and what he was doing to her. But he merely tightened his hold on her wrists, reminding her who was in charge. He was. Always. And she loved it.

He watched her face as he dragged the tips of his fingers along a sensitive patch of skin along her inner walls, and her legs began to shake. The pressure and friction increased on her clit, and the combined sensations had her splintering apart.

She wanted to scream from the pleasure rushing through her in waves, but she couldn't. So, instead, she closed her eyes and silently shuddered against the hand and fingers playing her so expertly and enjoyed the rest of the ride straight into bliss.

Chapter Twelve

FOR THE NEXT five days, Levi accompanied Sarah to and from work, and she was never left alone. If, for some reason, he couldn't keep an eye on her, one of his brothers did. It had to be that way until he knew for certain that Dylan was no longer a threat. Except there was no telling how long that would be.

Levi and Sarah had settled into a pattern at home. He'd never had a woman spend time at his place, but he discovered that he truly enjoyed having Sarah around, and he was quickly getting used to having her in his life on a daily basis. Going to bed with her every night, waking up together in the morning, and sharing meals and easy conversation were becoming a comfortable routine he looked forward to.

With him on leave for at least another week, they spent their days out—at a movie, lunch, or even a walk on Navy Pier or along Chicago's lakefront trail—anything to keep her mind distracted until her shift started at Kincaid's for the evening. He'd even treated her to a sundae at Ghirardelli's in the city, a place she'd always wanted to go to as a kid but had never had the opportunity.

Seeing her relaxed, laughing and smiling and gazing at him so affectionately, only solidified his growing feelings for her and made him more determined than ever to show her how perfectly she fit into his life, in so many ways. He'd never believed he'd settle down with just one person, never thought there would ever be a woman who understood not only his personal quirks but also his painful past. But Sarah accepted him, damaged past, flaws, and all.

Having been a waitress a few times before, she'd made an easy transition to the bar. She was efficient, competent, great with customers, and every night she'd come home with a good amount in tip money— far more than she was making at Circle K. He knew she was squirreling that cash away, and for now he let her, because there was no sense in arguing over wanting her to remain in Chicago with him when she still felt threatened by Dylan. Undoubtedly, a conversation like that would only push her away and make her more guarded. All he could do was show her how much she meant to him and how much he cared.

So far, Nick didn't have much to report on Dylan. The guy used a post office box for any mail delivery, and his last known physical address had been an apartment he no longer lived at. Which meant he was probably residing solely at the Sacrosanct compound.

Levi had made his own calls and contacts at the Eighteenth District Police Department, where they had jurisdiction over Fairdale, to find out what they knew about the supposed community. Come to find out, Sacrosanct was already involved in a lengthy and ongoing investigation with the FBI and ATF for suspected weapons violations. They'd already issued a search warrant and thoroughly inspected the grounds and spoken with the members. The two agencies had even brought Rick, the leader of the group, in for an interview but had found nothing they could use to shut the place down.

If there was any wrongdoing going on, the community hid it well.

But none of that news meant that Sarah was safe, and every day that passed made Levi feel tenser about the situation.

Tonight, he was sitting on a stool at the far end of the bar at Kincaid's in what had become his usual spot. He'd traded in his normal orange juice for a Sprite and lime, which had been Tara's suggestion to shake things up, she'd teased him. As he nursed the drink, he kept his gaze on the Sunday evening crowd. It was the slowest day of the week but still busy enough to keep Sarah's section full of customers.

"Everything still status quo?"

Levi pulled his gaze away from the main part of the bar, where the tables and dance floor were located, and glanced at his brother Mason, who slid onto the seat next to his. Over the last couple of nights, it had been Clay who'd hung out with Levi, not that he needed any backup when both his brothers had women at home they could be spending their time with. But it was nice to know they cared enough about Sarah, and what was going on with her, to keep themselves involved, even if it was just to keep him company for an hour or two while he waited for her shift to end.

"Nothing new to report," Levi confirmed as he took another drink of his Sprite.

His brother gave him a lopsided smile and nudged the elbow Levi had braced on the bar. "That's a good thing, right?"

"Yeah. But it's frustrating, too," he admitted, and when Mason gave him a curious look, he elaborated. "It's this stupid catch-twenty-two feeling of wanting something to happen so it can just be over for Sarah so she can put this entire incident behind her, and dreading it *being* over."

Mason smirked, his eyes glittering with amusement. "Damn, I'm having a hard time believing that Mr. Cool, Calm, and Collected has fallen in love, though it's nice to know you're human, after all, beneath all that straight-laced control," he joked.

Levi ignored Mason's wisecrack and instead frowned at him as he focused on the first part of that sentence. "I never said I was in love with Sarah."

"Are you saying you aren't?" Mason countered with a raised brow. "Because if that's the case, I'm going to have to call you out for being a fucking liar."

Levi blinked at Mason, stunned by the fact that his sibling—who'd once thought of *love* as a dirty word—was now suddenly an expert on Levi's emotions. He would have called out Mason for being a dick, but the thing was, his brother was actually being *sincere* in his encouragement, and that in itself was a shocking change, too.

Levi narrowed his gaze at Mason. "Who the hell are you, and what have you done with my self-centered, asshole brother?"

Mason chuckled, not at all offended by Levi's comment, not when they'd spent most of their adult lives antagonizing one another. "Blame Katrina," he said with a sappy grin that told Levi just how whipped his brother truly was. "I know it sounds trite and corny, but she's made me a better man. But I have to admit that I still have my asshole moments, so don't go thinking I'm a total pussy."

Levi laughed. Yeah, his brother was a changed man, for the better, thanks to the woman who'd stuck by his side for twelve long years as his best friend. Katrina and Mason were made for each other, like two pieces of a puzzle that fit perfectly together. Exactly the same way he felt about Sarah . . . *but love?* He cared deeply for her, and their connection was far more intense than anything he'd ever experienced, but honestly, Levi was afraid to believe it could really be true.

His heart pounded hard and fast in his chest as he glanced from the man who'd just sat down at the opposite end of the bar by himself and ordered a drink from Tara, to Mason. "What makes you think I'm in love with her?"

Mason rolled his eyes. "Jesus Christ, and here I thought *I* was dense when it came to my feelings for Katrina. Here's a simple question for you. Are you willing to let her walk out of your life and never see her again once this is all over?"

His answer was immediate, because he'd already thought about the possibility of Sarah leaving him once she knew she was safe, and it made his gut twist with turmoil. "No."

Mason tapped a few fingers on the top of the bar. "In order to keep her, are you prepared to offer Sarah something more than whatever this temporary arrangement between the two of you is?"

"Yes." Another automatic reply he didn't need to contemplate, even as he watched Sarah deliver a tray of drinks to a couple at a table, then switched his gaze back to the man at the end of the bar who kept glancing over his shoulder to look at something . . . or someone. "Of course."

"Like . . . forever?" Mason asked, very seriously.

Yes. The realization made him breathless, because *forever* meant the rest of his life. And Jesus Christ, he wanted that with Sarah. He wanted to give her everything she'd been robbed of since the death of her family. Everything she deserved and more. He wanted to take care of her, protect her, and yes, *love her.*

"Oh, fuck," he breathed in shock, and awe as well.

He loved Sarah.

"Ahhh, the light bulb finally went on." Mason grinned knowingly. "Both Clay and I have seen the way you look at her, the way you've upended your own life to help her when you've never done that for any other woman. We recognized the signs before you did because we've both been there. You just have to figure out the rest for yourself."

Levi already had, he realized. His biggest hurdle, he knew, was convincing a woman who believed she wasn't worthy of being loved that she was adored and cherished and special, and always would be. She'd spent most of her life being abandoned by people she trusted and believing that she wasn't good enough. He was going to do whatever it took to convince her otherwise, because he wasn't letting her go, *ever*, without a fight. *She was his.*

Levi met his brother's gaze and didn't miss the cocky expression on Mason's face. Funny how the tables had turned. How his brother—a totally re-formed man-whore—was now giving Levi advice about love.

Out of the corner of his eye, Levi saw the guy he'd been watching at the far end of the bar slide off his stool and head back toward where the restrooms were located. Nothing unusual for many of the patrons in the bar, but the fact that the guy was alone made Levi more suspicious than usual. He didn't think Sarah's ex would be bold and brave enough to make a move on her in public, but as a cop, Levi had seen and learned that desperate people did very stupid things without thinking through the consequences.

He had no idea what Dylan looked like, and he didn't think Sarah had seen the man's face when she came up to the service bar to collect her drink orders. She was so busy Levi knew she wasn't aware of her surroundings beyond her own customers, which wasn't a good thing at all.

But that's exactly why Levi was here, and as he saw the man leave the restroom, he narrowed his gaze, his body instinctively on edge as he watched every move the other guy made. He didn't like the way he stood off to the side in a shadowy corner or the way he was watching Sarah so intently.

"You got your eye on that guy who just came out of the men's room, too?" Mason asked in a low voice that was equally tense.

"Yep." Clearly, his brother was feeling the same apprehensive vibe that Levi was. Trusting his intuition, he slid off the barstool. "How about we go and ask him a few questions?"

"I'm in." Never one to pass up a good confrontation, Mason flexed his shoulders and fell into step beside Levi.

As they started in the man's direction, Sarah headed the same way to deliver a full tray of empty glasses to the bar, oblivious to anything except where she was going. She rounded the corner way before Levi could get there, and the guy abruptly stepped right in front of Sarah, causing the tray of glasses to fly from her hand and crash to the floor. Glass shattered every-where—the sound barely heard above the music playing in the bar.

All Levi saw was Sarah's round, horrified eyes as the man who had to be Dylan wrapped an arm around her waist and began hauling her back down the hallway—toward the back exit. As soon as she opened her mouth, Dylan clapped his hand over her lips to stifle her scream.

Adrenaline rushed through Levi's veins as he bolt-ed toward Sarah, with Mason following. There was so much going on around them that none of the patrons even noticed that Sarah had been grabbed. He felt the crunch of glass beneath his shoes, heard Tara yell something from the service bar, but didn't stop his pursuit. Once he cleared the main bar area where all the customers were, he withdrew his service revolver from the holster beneath his shirt, but before he could say or do anything, Dylan pushed open the delivery door and dragged Sarah out back with him.

"*Fuck*." Levi ran after them, bursting through the door to find Dylan standing close to a beat-up Toyota, now facing Levi with a knife at Sarah's throat. Levi came to an abrupt stop but kept his gun trained on Dylan's head, the only part of his body Levi could see. The motion detector light had come on, and the panic he saw in Sarah's eyes nearly destroyed him, but he managed to keep his cool. He had to put his emotions aside in order to think clearly and rationally.

Vaguely he realized that Mason hadn't followed

him out, that Levi was on his own. *Where the fuck had his brother gone?* "Let her go, Dylan," Levi ordered.

"The only place she's going is with me," the other man yelled back as the knife shook under Sarah's chin. "She's mine, and I'm taking her back where she belongs!"

"She doesn't want to go back to Sacrosanct," Levi said very clearly, just as he saw a figure come around the building behind Dylan and move quietly toward the other man. *Mason.* Thank God.

"Doesn't matter what she wants."

Sarah made a soft sound of distress. Dylan must have tightened his hold, and Levi's gut twisted, and he exhaled a harsh breath. As a cop, he'd been trained to negotiate during a standoff, to diffuse the situation before it escalated to violence. Right now, it took every ounce of control Levi possessed to follow procedure, instead of acting on pure instinct and shooting the guy between the eyes.

"Think about what you're doing, Dylan." He caught another movement as Mason crouched and eased around the car where Dylan was standing. "If you kidnap Sarah and try to take her back, you're going with a police escort."

"If you don't put your fucking gun down, I'm going to slit her throat!" Dylan yelled, as if he hadn't heard Levi or just didn't care. "Do it *now*!"

The other man waved the knife in the air in a threatening gesture. With the blade away from Sarah's throat, Mason snuck up and grabbed Dylan's arm, the one holding the weapon, and quickly twisted it behind his back, so high and hard that the man screamed in pain and automatically released the knife, letting go of Sarah.

Once freed, she stumbled toward Levi. He grasped her hand and pulled her behind him just as Mason wrenched both of Dylan's arms behind his back, pinning them tight.

Threat disabled, Levi holstered his gun, and as much as he wanted to take a frightened Sarah in his arms and reassure both her and himself that she was fine, they weren't done with Dylan just yet.

Levi glanced at Sarah and gave her a reassuring glance. "Stay right here," he said and then approached Dylan.

Even though Mason had Dylan immobilized, the other man still tried to come at Levi, but Mason's hold was so strong and unrelenting Dylan's struggles barely registered.

Levi stopped in front of the furious man, who looked just as enraged as Levi felt at the moment.

"Listen to me," Levi said, his jaw clenching. "Sarah is not going anywhere with you. Not now. Not *ever*. If you come near her again, you'll be sorry that you did."

"Fuck you!" Dylan spat.

Levi shifted his gaze to Mason's, the smirk on his brother's face indicating Mason was itching for a fight, before he glanced at Dylan. "I suggest you get in your car, go back to wherever you came from, and stay there."

"Not without Sarah."

The man was persistent, he'd give him that. But Levi had warned him. "Then I guess we'll just have to change your mind about that."

Instead of bothering with the prick himself, Levi walked over to where Sarah was still standing, her arms crossed over her chest, her body trembling, and pulled her against him, relieved to finally hold her, knowing she was safe.

Levi looked over his shoulder just as Mason said, "Okay, asshole, let's knock some sense into that hard head of yours. Maybe you'll understand just how serious we are about you not going near Sarah ever again."

Mason let go of Dylan, who predictably turned around, throwing the first angry punch in Mason's direction—which Levi knew his brother was hoping for. Anticipating the assault, Mason stopped it with his forearm and used his other hand to deliver a blow to Dylan's stomach that had him doubling over before attempting to charge at Mason once again. Stupid move, considering Mason had learned to fight on the mean streets where they'd grown up.

The brawl was on, and there wasn't a doubt in Levi's mind that Mason would take care of Sarah's problem and work Dylan over until he convinced the asshole to stay away. Sarah didn't need to stay and watch the beatdown, not when she was so visibly shaken. Gently grabbing her arm, he turned her away from the bloodbath about to ensue and led her back inside the bar.

Tara rushed up to him, clearly panicked. "I didn't know if you wanted me to call 911 or if you wanted to handle the situation yourself, so I didn't call the police."

"Perfect," he said, noticing that someone had cleaned up the shattered glasses from the floor. "Mason is getting rid of the garbage out back, and consider Sarah off work for the rest of the night. I'm taking her home."

"Of course," Tara said, understanding in her tone.

Sarah was silent as he guided her out to his truck, probably still in shock, and remained so on the drive home. He didn't want to bombard her with questions just yet, not when his own emotions were churning inside of him, ranging from fear of seeing her so vulnerable with yet another weapon threatening her life to anger that *anyone* dare to try and hurt her, to a rush of possessiveness that had threatened his control like nothing ever before.

They arrived at his place, and she walked through the kitchen to the dining room, still much too quiet and subdued. His entire body felt as though he were going to splinter apart at the thought of nearly losing Sarah, of Dylan either driving off with her or using that blade to prove some kind of deranged point.

"Sarah," he said just as she reached the dining table.

She turned around, the lost, painful look in her eyes so damned heartbreaking he could barely stand it.

He closed the distance between them and rubbed his hands up and down her arms. "Are you okay?" he asked gruffly.

"I'm fine," she said in a barely audible voice. "But I think it's time for me to go."

He didn't have to ask *where*. He already knew the answer, that nothing had changed and she was following through on her plans to get out of the city. Dread tightened in his chest.

Her eyes filled with tears. "This is what happens when people are around me," she said in a raspy voice. "I always seem to attract trouble, and you're such a great guy, you deserve someone who has her life together. You deserve someone so much better than me."

He could feel her physically pulling away from him, withdrawing. He processed her words, saw the yearning in her eyes that contradicted everything she'd just said, and wondered if her reasons for walking away from him ran much deeper than the excuses she'd just given him.

He trusted what they could have together, what they could *build* together, but knew that she'd been burned by hopeful relationships before. It was *her* inability to believe that she was worthy of being loved that was keeping her from staying with him.

"I love you," he said without hesitation, because if that's what it took for her to remain right here with him, in his house, in his life, then he was putting every-fucking-thing on the table.

She sucked in a breath, the fear in her eyes unmistakable. "You can't," she said in an aching voice.

He held her face in his hands to make sure she couldn't look away from him. "I can, and I do. I don't care about your past, Sarah. I only care about us, and a future together."

She made an inarticulate sound, one that was wrapped up with doubts and denial. Desperation surged through him, along with a possessive emotion he couldn't contain. Right here, right now, he didn't want to hold back anything with Sarah. Tomorrow morning, it would be soon enough for them to hash out her fears, because there was no fucking way he was letting her walk out his door without a down and dirty fight. It just wasn't going to happen.

Threading his fingers into her hair, he brought her mouth to his and kissed her, hard and deep, until she softened beneath the onslaught of his lips and tongue and joined in with her own frantic abandon. She thought this was the last time they'd be together, but he was going to make damn sure it was just the beginning.

Her hands tugged at the hem of his T-shirt, and he let her pull it over his head while yanking hers off, too. As they made their way toward his bedroom, the rest of their clothes were haphazardly removed. Both of them naked, he pressed her down onto his bed, reached for a condom and sheathed himself, then settled between her spread legs.

This wasn't about foreplay and fun. This was about

claiming her, branding her, *loving her.* It was about stripping things down physically so she'd allow him in emotionally. He wouldn't accept anything less.

He stroked the head of his cock through her wet folds and pushed into her, just enough that she knew what was about to happen, and that's all the warning he gave her. The first driving thrust had her crying out in pleasure. The second had the sound of her sweet, unyielding moan echoing in his ears. After that, heat and desire blended together, creating an inferno of need that had them both straining against one another as he drove deeper and deeper inside her.

He didn't hold her down. Didn't restrain her hands. He gave her all the freedom she could ever want to touch him, to make her own demands, and strip away all his defenses so there was no doubt in her mind how serious he was about her. About them.

Things turned wild and uncontrolled quickly, and he welcomed her unbridled response, too. She wrapped her legs tight around his waist and raked her fingers down his spine—marking him, based on the sting of pain along his skin. He exhaled on a hiss of breath as need and passion entwined, shoving him closer to the edge.

He delved all ten fingers into her silky hair and tipped her head back. Her lips parted, and her dark, stormy blue eyes latched on to his, exposing her emotions, her desires. "This is where I belong, Sarah," he said raggedly, slamming his body against hers, again and again. "Right here, with you. Inside you."

Her expression exposed every one of her vulnerabilities, including her true and honest feelings for him. "Yes," she whispered, and that one word sent them both free-falling into the sweet depths of exquisite pleasure.

Chapter Thirteen

SARAH WOKE UP in a now familiar position . . .
snuggled up to Levi with him holding her securely
in his embrace. Morning light from outside was
starting to stream into the room through the window,
but she didn't move. She didn't want to disturb Levi,
and she wanted time to process everything that had
happened last night now that her head was clear and
her thoughts were no longer clouded by panic and
fear.

She wasn't surprised that Dylan had found her.
She'd been more shocked that he'd been bold
enough—and stupid enough—to try and abduct her
right at work. He'd never been the brightest guy, and
his actions last night had proved as much.

She couldn't deny that she was grateful that both
Levi and Mason had been there to diffuse the situation, to make sure that she was protected to the best
of their ability. She owed them both for keeping her

safe when things could have ended much differently.

Was she still worried that Dylan would come after her again? A part of her was concerned, yes, because it was always a possibility, and there were no guarantees. But during the course of the night, she'd kept wondering what it would be like to stay with Levi, to stop running and just live life happily. To be a part of his family and finally feel as though she'd found a place where she belonged. More than anything in the world, she wanted that. She wanted Levi. *And he loved her.*

Remembering his emotional confession stole the breath from her lungs. Now that she wasn't overwhelmed with anxiety, her heart acknowledged that admission, and she didn't doubt his sincerity for a second. Levi was honest and real, a man who stayed true to his word—something she'd seen firsthand.

Closing her eyes, she inhaled his now familiar scent and listened to his steady breathing. Her past was filled with people she'd trusted who'd rejected and disappointed her. Who'd made promises that they'd never followed through on that left her devastated. It had become a recurring pattern in her life, something she'd come to expect and anticipate. Even with Levi, and that hadn't been a fair comparison when she'd never given him a real chance.

Even as she'd tried to push him away over the past six weeks since initially meeting him, Levi had refused to accept defeat. He'd persisted, even after taking a bullet for her. He'd given her a place to stay—insisted, actually—after discovering where and how she lived.

He'd protected her when he learned about Dylan. Not once did he make her feel like an inconvenience, and most importantly, he didn't give up on her, not even last night when she'd panicked and shunned his declaration of love.

Instead, he'd *showed her* how much he cared, how much he wanted her, how emotionally invested he was in her. In them.

She swallowed hard, realizing she was at the most important crossroad of her life. She could leave and walk away from Levi because she was too afraid to believe he wanted her in all the ways that mattered, or she could stay and open her heart to all the possibilities that lay ahead of her with this amazing man supporting her.

This time, there were no fears complicating her decision. No doubts or hesitations or confusion. No, her feelings came to her with such clarity, she knew that she loved him, as well. How could she not, when he was the best man she'd ever known, despite his own messed-up childhood? If he could open his heart to her after everything he'd been through, then she was willing to take that chance with him, as well.

She just hoped that she wasn't too late after her adverse reaction to his declaration last night.

The ringing of the doorbell startled her, and beside her, Levi roused ever-so-slightly. It was only eight in the morning, and she couldn't imagine who was there, unless it was someone from Levi's family.

A firm knock sounded, and Levi woke up completely. With a grumble and a curse, he rolled out of bed, put on a pair of sweat pants, and walked out of the bedroom without a shirt on and his hair disheveled from her fingers twisting in the strands last night.

Curious to know who was at the door, she slid out of bed, too, and put on one of Levi's T-shirts that was long enough to fall to mid-thigh. As she walked down the hallway, she heard two male voices—Levi's, and . . . another familiar one. Rick, the leader of Sacrosanct.

Her skin prickled with trepidation, her knees went weak, and she pressed her back against the nearest wall so she didn't collapse to the floor. Her heart pounded hard in her chest, and she strained to hear their conversation, which started with Rick introducing himself in that pleasant way of his that had always made her feel distinctly uncomfortable, though he'd never hurt her, personally.

"How did you find my place?" Levi demanded to know, his voice sharp and authoritative. "And what the fuck do you want? If you're here for Sarah, you'll have to get through me first, and I can pretty much guarantee that you won't get very far."

"I found your place because, like you, I have my sources. And I'm not here for Sarah, or to issue threats," Rick said in a calm, placating tone of voice. "But to reassure you that Dylan will no longer be bothering her. He can be a bit . . . obsessive, and I just found out from one of my assistants that he's been harassing her."

"Damn fucking straight he's been harassing her," Levi said, not doing anything to subdue his anger. "In fact, he threatened to take her back to Sacrosanct, where she was held against her will."

"That had to be some kind of mistake." Once again, the leader's tone was modulated, as it always was. "We don't hold people against their will. Our main gates are always locked, but everyone is free to come and go as they please."

"I'm gonna have to call bullshit on that, considering I know all about the ongoing investigation with the FBI and ATF," Levi said, sarcasm lacing his deep voice as he acknowledged what he was already privy to. "But right now, all I care about is that Sarah is completely left alone."

"I understand. I don't want any problems, either, or another investigation."

Which was exactly why Rick had made a personal appearance, Sarah knew.

The leader continued. "Your brother made his point with Dylan last night," he said meaningfully, letting Levi know that he was well aware of what had gone down at Kincaid's. "We just picked Dylan up, and he's being put on probation and will be transferred to another community. He won't be back."

"I don't even want to know what any of that means," Levi replied. "But if he does come back, I can guarantee I will rain the wraths of hell down on you and your community."

"Duly noted."

The conversation ended, and Sarah heard the front door close. She stepped out around the corner, and Levi stopped in his tracks when he saw her, his gaze immediately turning cautious.

"I heard everything," she said before he could ask.

Levi slowly closed the distance between them, shaking his head. "Is he always so . . . agreeable?"

"He doesn't want to draw any negative attention to the community, so in this case, yes. I'm sure he's trying to cover his ass since you're a cop."

"Too late." Levi grinned. "Trust me, it's just a matter of time before ATF is *up* his ass again. From the things I heard from my contact at the Eighteenth District PD, Rick and his community won't be around for long."

Levi stared at Sarah, his gaze searching hers, as if looking for answers to everything that had transpired last night. He looked nervous, and she understood why. He was anticipating that this morning was going to be the end of them.

She put him out of his misery. "I'm not going anywhere, Levi."

He didn't look as reassured as she'd thought he would, and his expression remained tentative. "What does that mean, exactly?"

She gave him a soft smile. "It means that I'm staying right here, with you, despite my fears and hang-ups because of my past."

"Sweetheart, we all have hang-ups." He gently brushed her hair away from her cheek. "All I want is for you to give us a chance, and that's something I've never asked another woman to do, and you want to know why?"

The emotion shining in his eyes was unlike anything that had ever been directed solely at her, and it was so easy to bask in his affection. "Why?"

"Because you are everything I need in my life, but didn't know until you were a part of it," he stated simply. "For five weeks, I pursued you because there was something about *you* that I wasn't willing to give up on. Something so sweet and genuine, and then I discovered how similar our pasts were, and it all made so much sense why I was drawn to you. I've shared things with you that no one else knows, not even my brothers. I want to share *everything* with you."

She closed her eyes for a moment, wondering if she ought to pinch herself to make sure that this was all real. That Levi was real and not some figment of her imagination. When she opened them, the answer was right in front of her, smiling at her with hope in his eyes and his heart on his sleeve—proving that everything about this moment was real, and she wanted it all with him.

She smiled back at him. "I love you, Levi Kincaid."

He blinked at her in surprise. "Yeah?" he asked huskily, though there was a distinct happiness in his eyes that warmed her from the inside out.

"Yes." She wrapped her arms around his neck and pulled him down for a kiss, and for the first time in a very long time, everything felt perfect and right.

Chapter Fourteen

One month later . . .

LEVI WAS A man in love. That was something he'd never believed he'd ever have, but one single woman made it all possible. Sarah Robins. She'd changed his life, and as he glanced at her as she sat beside him while they watched Mason and Katrina get married in Clay and Samantha's backyard, he knew he'd changed her life, too. Somehow, two broken, damaged people with screwed-up pasts had found one another and had managed to make each other whole.

Sarah was watching the ceremony with big, wide eyes, listening as vows were spoken and rings were exchanged. She was stunningly beautiful in a peach lace dress that skimmed the curves gradually filling out her body, thanks to the meals he cooked, and her blonde hair was a bit shorter now, but silky and shiny.

But most of all, she looked relaxed, happy, and

content. She was no longer the timid woman he'd originally met at the convenience store. She was more vibrant, more confident, and he loved seeing those changes in her because it only made their relationship stronger, on every level.

He'd gotten a clean bill of health and was back to work patrolling the streets of Chicago. Since he still worked swing shift—something he was trying to change to spend more time with Sarah—she insisted on waitressing at Kincaid's to help with any expenses even though he'd told her it wasn't necessary. But at least he knew she was in a safe and protected environment, and she truly enjoyed being around her new friends and family.

But what Levi was proudest of was the fact that she'd decided to go back to school to pursue her nursing degree, which was something she'd wanted to do for a long time. Now, she could, with his full support.

Everything between the two of them seemed to be falling into place nicely, but as he watched Mason smile at his new bride with the biggest, dorkiest, happiest grin on his face when he was announced as her husband, Levi knew that there was still one more thing he wanted in his life. He hated to be selfish when he had so much to be thankful for, but he wanted Sarah as his wife, not just his girlfriend. He needed to give her that promise of forever and reassure her that they were in this for the long haul together. He planned to make it happen, but he was just a little nervous about whether or not *she* was ready to take that next step in their relationship.

He'd find out soon enough.

The ceremony ended, and Mason and Katrina walked out into the small gathering of people who'd been invited to help celebrate their nuptials. The day's celebration was an intimate but informal affair, with just family and close friends present—seventeen people in all. Mason had worn a white dress shirt with a purple-hued tie to match the tips of Katrina's blonde hair, and a pair of dark trousers. The bride had opted for a knee-length, strapless white dress that showed off the colorful butterflies covering her arm. Katrina couldn't look more beautiful and happy, and Mason, well, that cocky expression on his face said it all.

Everyone gathered around the bride and groom as Mason poured champagne into each of their glasses for a toast, bypassing Levi, who was holding a glass of water for obvious reasons. When Mason reached Samantha, she already had a glass of water in her hand, as well.

Mason frowned at her. "Seriously, Samantha? Are you becoming a teetotaler like Levi? It's my wedding and the champagne is freakin' expensive, so have a drink."

Samantha glanced at Clay, then back at Mason with an impish smile. "I really can't. It's not good for the baby."

Mason gave her an odd look of confusion. "The baby . . ." Then it dawned on him and his eyes grew wide in shock. "*Holy shit*, you're having a baby!"

"We are," Clay confirmed proudly.

"Oh, my God!" Katrina squealed happily, clearly not caring that the attention was suddenly on someone else. "This is the best news *ever*! Mason is going to be an uncle, and I'm going to be an aunt!"

"Congratulations," Sarah said as she gave Samantha a warm hug.

Levi shook his brother's hand, then leaned over and kissed his sister-in-law on the cheek. "I'm so happy for both of you."

"Thanks, man." Clay met Levi's gaze, and for a moment, they shared a look that commiserated on how far they'd all come, how much they'd all changed, all because of the right woman in their life. "It just feels right, you know?"

"Yeah, I know," Levi agreed, because he felt the same way about Sarah.

A toast was made to the newlyweds, then again to Clay and Samantha for their baby news. The atmosphere was festive, and even though there was only a small group of guests attending the wedding, Mason had gone all out with a high-end buffet of food and even a DJ for music. The celebration and happiness was infectious, and later in the evening, when a slow song was playing, Levi escorted Sarah out onto the dance floor and pulled her into his arms.

Like always, she came willingly, cuddling against his chest in the sweetest way possible. She laid her cheek on his chest and tucked her head beneath his chin, her entire body relaxing completely against his as they swayed to the music.

"Are you having a good time?" he murmured into her ear.

She lifted her head and smiled up at him, her face wreathed with joy. "I'm having a great time. I love your family."

His heart seemed to expand inside his chest. "They love you, too. But not as much as I do, obviously."

Her eyes twinkled playfully. "Yeah, and how much is that?"

"I love you forever." And he was about to prove it.

They were at his brother's dinner reception, surrounded by loved ones, but for right now, Levi kept everything as private as possible, just between the two of them. Letting Sarah go, he moved back a step and withdrew the small black box he'd put into his pants pocket earlier. As soon as she saw it, she gasped and her hand flew to her mouth in shock. He merely smiled and popped open the lid to reveal a sparkling engagement ring he'd had designed just for her. In that magical moment, every anxiety faded, and certainty settled over him.

"Sarah Robins, will you marry me? You make me whole and complete and—"

"Yes!" she said, interrupting him. "I want nothing more than to marry you!"

He pushed the ring on her finger, and it was a perfect fit. Just like she was. Pulling her back into his arms, he kissed her, then whispered in her ear.

"You know what this means, don't you?" When she gave him a questioning look, he grinned down at her and said, "You're going to be cuffed to me for life."

She laughed and hugged him tight. "There's no place I'd rather be."

Epilogue

TARA KENT CAST a quick glance at the small clock behind the bar. Another half hour and Kincaid's would be open for business. Other employees were gradually arriving for work, and prep for the evening crowd was underway. She checked her liquor inventory and made sure the bins were filled with ice, then set out the garnish trays over at the service area of the bar.

Out of the corner of her eye, she saw someone walk into the bar through the front door that was left unlocked, and she glanced up, expecting to see one of the bar waitresses arriving for her shift. As soon as she caught sight of a man in a business suit, she automatically said, "I'm sorry, but we don't open until four."

Then she looked at his face and confusion washed over her. At first glance, the man looked *exactly* like Clay. The strong, chiseled features were the same, as were the stunning blue eyes and full, sensual lips. She'd always had a crush on her boss, but she'd never acted on it, but damn, she'd never seen him in a suit be-fore—and this one looked like an expensive custom-made number—and he looked sexy as hell.

Heat and awareness settled low and deep in her belly, shocking her. What. The. Hell? Clay was married to Samantha, who Tara absolutely adored, *so where had that physical reaction come from to a man who was taken and whom she'd known for the past few years?*

She blinked and looked closer, and then she started seeing subtle differences. Not just the high-dollar suit but the cut of this man's hair was shorter than Clay's, and the way he carried himself was dynamic and powerful and confident in a way that screamed wealth, intelligence, and success. His shoulders weren't quite as wide, but he was trim and fit, and she suddenly wanted to know what he looked like beneath the tailored jacket and crisp white shirt he wore.

She swallowed to ease the dryness in her throat, and when she finally lifted her gaze to his gorgeous face, she didn't miss the flicker of amusement in his eyes or the smile playing around the corners of his sensual lips—as if he was in on a secret that she wasn't. And she suddenly had a feeling she knew what that secret was.

She shook her head and managed, somehow, to gather her wits enough to speak. "You're not Clay . . . "

"No, I'm not," he said in a low, husky voice that made her think of sex and sin, with him. "I'm his twin brother, Jackson Stone."

Next up:
DIRTY SEXY SINNER
(Jackson Stone's story)!

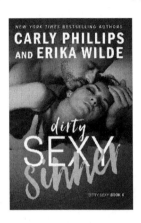

Thank you for reading DIRTY SEXY CUFFED. We would appreciate it if you would help others enjoy this book too. Please recommend to others and leave a review.

Sign up for Carly Phillips & Erika Wilde's Newsletters:

Carly's Newsletter
http://smarturl.it/CarlysNewsletter

Erika's Newsletter
http://smarturl.it/ErikaWildeNewsletter

Dirty Sexy Series Reading Order:
Dirty Sexy Saint (Clay Kincaid)
Dirty Sexy Inked (Mason Kincaid)
Dirty Sexy Cuffed (Levi Kincaid)
Dirty Sexy Sinner (Jackson Stone)
*Every book in the Dirty Sexy series can be read alone for your reading enjoyment!

Read on for Excerpts of Carly & Erika's books:
DARE TO TAKE by Carly Phillips
PLAYING WITH TEMPTATION by Erika Wilde

Dare to Take

Excerpt

by Carly Phillips

THE SUN SHONE overhead, the temperature neared ninety, and the humidity was hair-curlingly high on the Caribbean island of St. Lucia, making it hard to believe a hurricane was coming soon. Ella Shaw glanced up at the blue sky, knowing it wouldn't remain pristine for long.

The calm before the storm.

She pulled her hair into a high ponytail and headed out of her hotel, determined to hit the local gift shop she'd caught sight of on her way to the photo shoot yesterday. She'd seen long, draping, blue-beaded necklaces from the storefront window, but she hadn't had time to stop. Her boss was a stickler for getting the right shot in the exact light, and they'd worked well past dark. By the time they'd wrapped for the day, the store had been closed.

As an assistant for Angie Crighton, a fashion designer based in Miami, Ella was responsible for the little details involved in a photo shoot. And though Angie, the photographer, and models had left the island this morning, Ella had stayed to make sure the shooting site was clean, the hotel pleased enough to allow them back another time. And if she were honest with herself, she liked the downtime after the craziness of a photo shoot, the rushing around of the crew, the bossiness of some of the models and, of course, of Angie herself.

Ella appreciated the fact that she had time to souvenir shop for her best friend, Avery Dare. How ironic was it that the two girls from very different worlds had met at all? But they had. And it was Avery who'd introduced Ella to the finer things in life, leading her to seek out a job with an haute-couture designer. Whereas Avery came from a wealthy family, Ella had been raised firmly middle class, but the two girls had bonded instantly. They'd even shared an apartment until recently, when her best friend had moved in with her rock star boyfriend, Grey Kingston.

Yep, two different worlds, even now, Ella thought wryly. But their friendship was solid. Which reminded her, she needed to let Avery know she might not make it back to the States tomorrow as planned.

When Ella had heard about the storm changing course, she'd tried to book an earlier flight out, without success. She shivered at the possibility of being stranded here alone during a hurricane and knew Avery would like the news even less. Her best friend suffered from severe anxiety, and Ella didn't like to make her worry.

She'd just buy Avery an extra gift to make up for it,

she thought, walking into the shop. She immediately headed to the turquoise-blue beads she'd seen through the window. The shopkeeper claimed they were Larimar beads. Even if they were fake, the beads, popular in the Caribbean, were said to have healing powers. Ella purchased two dozen, a mix of bracelets and necklaces, so she could share with the children at the cancer treatment center where she and Avery volunteered.

Avery had been nine, Ella ten years old when they'd met at a Miami hospital, both donating bone marrow, both there at the behest of a parent. Neither of them really understanding what was happening. All Ella had known was that she was doing a favor for her father, helping the stepmother Ella didn't like all that much to begin with. Even at a young age, Ella had been a good judge of character, a better one than her father, obviously, because shortly after Janice had gotten well, she'd left Ella's dad. And both her father and Ella's life had gone downhill from there. Ella shook off the thoughts of her past before she could go deeper and darker, and focused on the pretty jewelry.

She spent some time choosing a thick turquoise bracelet for Avery and a similar one for herself before paying for everything and waiting for the shopkeeper to wrap things up.

Bag in hand, she started back to the hotel, cutting through side streets and looking into the windows of the stores, soaking up the culture along the cobblestone streets before heading back to Miami tomorrow.

At least, she still hoped she'd be home. Knowing she couldn't change the outcome, she pushed her worrisome thoughts aside. She'd deal with the situation as it came.

Sweat dampened her neck from the humidity of the island, and she contemplated taking a cab back to the hotel. She reached into her straw bag and pulled out her cell phone to make the call, when, without warning, she felt a hard jerk on her purse.

"What the—?" She spun around, but whomever wanted her purse was quicker.

She barely caught a glimpse of a tall guy with dark hair as he yanked harder, nearly pulling her shoulder out of its socket before slamming her against the nearby building with his other hand.

Her head hit the concrete wall, and spots immediately appeared behind her eyes from the impact. As she struggled not to pass out, the man grabbed her purse, along with her cell phone that had fallen to the ground.

She opened her mouth to scream, but nothing came out. Her legs collapsed beneath her, and she fell to the ground, her head smacking the sidewalk before everything went black.

TYLER DARE HAD a full day planned, a packed schedule of appointments with existing and potential clients of Double Down Security, the firm he now co-owned with his brother Scott. Serena Gibson, his close friend and personal assistant, had strict orders not to let anyone interrupt him this morning so he could pull together his notes for each meeting.

He picked up the threat assessment sheet for his first client, a diplomat who needed protection for his family, and began to scan the findings, when he heard raised voices.

"I'm sorry, Avery, but he said no interruptions," Serena insisted.

"That's okay, I'm sure he'll see me." His sister's voice carried through the closed office door.

"Avery, he said not to let anyone inside." Serena's voice rose, but he knew the soft-spoken woman was no match for a determined Dare female.

Start Reading Dare to Take NOW!

Playing with Temptation
Excerpt
by Erika Wilde

RAINA BECK FINISHED helping a customer select a bottle of warming massage oil, then headed over to the lingerie section of her store, Sugar and Spice, a sensual, upscale adult boutique that catered to the residents of San Diego. She paused at the rack of new arrivals, where her good friend, Jillian Noble, was perusing the gorgeous items.

"Find anything you like?" Raina asked as the other woman contemplated a leopard-print bustier before putting it back on the stand.

Jillian smiled at her as she shuffled through a few more pieces. "The problem is, there's too much to like, which is a good thing. I'm looking for something a little different than everything I already have…" Her words trailed off, and her eyes lit up as she lifted a hanger displaying a sexy red ensemble that consisted of a demi bra, a short flirty skirt that was only a few inches of fabric that would barely cover her bottom, and a matching lace thong, along with a garter belt and thigh-high stockings.

"I think this is it," Jillian announced with a succinct nod of her head.

"If Dean comes home to find you wearing that outfit, I think all bets are off," Raina teased her friend.

"That's what I'm counting on, and I think he'll really like the short little skirt, too." She handed the hanger to Raina. "I'll take it, along with one of those feather ticklers you have on display, the one with the soft ostrich feathers."

"You got it." Raina smiled, knowing Jillian, a good customer, appreciated the more sexually adventurous items Sugar and Spice provided to those who wanted to kink up their sex lives. Selecting a tickler with deep red feathers to match the outfit, she met her friend up at the front counter.

As she rang up Jillian's purchases, she asked, "How are you enjoying working with Stephanie?"

"I absolutely love it. I couldn't be happier," Jillian said, her expression reflecting her newfound joy. "I'm helping her design those fantasy suites at the hotel, and tomorrow I have a consultation with a woman who wants to redecorate her bedroom in a sexier version theme of The Secret Garden theme."

"Sounds like a fun project." Raina swiped Jillian's credit card to process the sale. The two of them had become close friends over the past months, and because she knew Jillian's husband had been so opposed to his wife taking a job, Raina couldn't help but wonder how that was going. "Is everything still good with Dean and you working for Stephanie?"

"He's getting used to it and adjusting. I make sure I always make time for just the two of us, and it keeps him happy."

"Men really are such basic creatures," Raina said with a laugh. "Keep them plied with food and sex and they're happy, content, and satisfied."

Jillian lifted a curious brow. "Speaking of men and sex...when are *you* going to indulge a little?"

Raina shrugged as she wrapped her ensemble in pink tissue and tucked it into a bag. "I think all the good guys are taken. And then there's the men who find out I own a sex toy boutique and decide I'm fair game for outrageous, kinky sex, because, you know, I have access to all sorts of depraved items."

She rolled her eyes to make light of her comment, but the truth ran much deeper and stirred up other painful memories that reminded her of why she kept her heart and emotions under lock and key—the pain of such complete and utter rejection was something that had left her guarded and very cautious when it came to a man's interest in her.

Admittedly, she *did* enjoy hot, adventurous sex. After all, she'd opened Sugar and Spice as a way to help women empower themselves sexually, to get in touch with their desires and be confident enough to enjoy every aspect of sex. But she also knew it took an equally strong, self-assured man to accept her line of business, to not feel threatened or embarrassed by the fact that she owned a boutique that catered to enhancing sexual pleasure.

Unfortunately, over the years, she'd learned that she wasn't the best judge of character when it came to a man's motives and his reasons for dating her, which also made it extremely difficult to decipher what was *real*, or if she was nothing more than someone's dirty little secret that he used until the excitement wore off.

Too many painful experiences had taught her that because of what she did for a living, men were more than willing to fuck her like a porn star in private, but they drew the line at taking her out in public or bringing her home to meet the family, which made her feel cheap and dirty—as if her own father's fire and brimstone prediction about her being a whore had come true. Men didn't date *a woman like her* with long term in mind, and it had become much easier for Raina to keep her emotional distance rather than face criticism and the sting of rejection all over again.

She'd been burned a few times, and she wasn't allowing any man to get close enough to do it again. Now, sex was all about physical pleasure, nothing more, and she'd recently decided that if anyone was going to do the *using*, it was going to be *her* for a change. Unfortunately, an opportunity hadn't presented itself, but if the right guy came along, she certainly wasn't opposed to enjoying a no-strings-attached one-night stand.

"Maybe you need hot *anonymous* sex," Jillian suggested with a naughty twinkle in her eye, as if she'd had a direct link to Raina's thoughts.

"It's been a long dry spell and the idea is definitely

tempting," Raina replied, a humorous note lacing the truth of her words. Vibrators and sex toys did the job as far as getting her off, but they couldn't replace the feel or pleasure of a strong, powerful, virile man thrusting deep inside of her or skimming his hands along her curves, his hot mouth seducing hers.

Yes, she definitely missed that, and the provocative thought made her feel a bit flushed.

Jillian bit her bottom lip for a second before reaching into her purse and pulling out a white envelope. "You've done a lot for me, and I want to do something for you for a change. Take this, and indulge yourself." She pushed the envelope across the counter to Raina.

Raina picked it up and read the word *Welcome* embossed in black across the front. "What is this?" she asked, confused and curious at the same time.

"An invitation to The Players Club."

Raina's eyes widened in surprise, and her heart fluttered in her chest with undeniable excitement. She knew exactly what The Players Club was—a private, members-only sex club that catered to an elite and prominent clientele in order to maintain its exclusivity. A personal recommendation was required to even visit the club, and since Dean and Jillian had recently become members, they now had the privilege of extending an invitation to a guest.

And Jillian had chosen *her*.

"Oh, wow," Raina breathed as she brushed her thumb over the embossed lettering on the envelope, still in shock. "Really?"

"Yes, *really*," Jillian mimicked playfully. "You deserve a sexy night all to yourself, and I can guarantee that *any* fantasy you have can be fulfilled at The Players Club."

Raina had plenty of private, naughty fantasies stored away in the deepest recesses of her mind, none of which she'd ever shared because those scenarios were just too wicked and forbidden to reveal to any of the guys she'd dated up to this point, all of whom had big egos and had been self-centered lovers. Yes, she owned a boutique that sold all sorts of kinky items to enhance sex play, but it took a strong, confident man who didn't feel threatened by her expertise to give her what she desired, who knew what she needed without asking and made that pleasure his sole focus.

Finding that kind of compelling man at The Players Club in one night was improbable but certainly more possible than in her daily life, and she wasn't about to refuse Jillian's gift. She'd been given the equivalent of Willy Wonka's golden ticket, but instead of gorging on chocolate, she planned to indulge in as many orgasms as she could.

Start Reading Playing with Temptation NOW!

About the Authors

Carly Phillips

Carly Phillips is the *N.Y. Times* and *USA Today* Best-selling Author of over 50 sexy contemporary romance novels featuring hot men, strong women and the emotionally compelling stories her readers have come to expect and love. Carly is happily married to her college sweetheart, the mother of two nearly adult daughters and three crazy dogs (two wheaten terriers and one mutant Havanese) who star on her Facebook Fan Page and website. Carly loves social media and is always around to interact with her readers. You can find out more about Carly at www.carlyphillips.com.

Erika Wilde

Erika Wilde is the author of the sexy Marriage Diaries series and The Players Club series. She lives in Oregon with her husband and two daughters, and when she's not writing you can find her exploring the beautiful Pacific Northwest. For more information on her upcoming releases, please visit website at www. erikawilde.com.

Made in the USA
Middletown, DE
18 September 2016